HOCKEY NIGHT IN
THE ROUGH TOWNS

HOCKEY NIGHT IN THE ROUGH TOWNS

By

Jerold Wadsworth

Library and Archives Canada Cataloguing in Publication

Title: Hockey night in the rough towns / by Jerold Wadsworth.

Names: Wadsworth, Jerold author

Description: Short stories.

Identifiers: Canadiana (print) 20190086505 | Canadiana (ebook) 20190086513 | ISBN 9781771614511 (softcover) | ISBN 9781771614528 (HMTL) | ISBN 9781771614535 (Kindle) | ISBN 9781771614542 (PDF)

Classification: LCC PS8645.A34 H63 2019 | DDC C813/.6—dc23

Published by Mosaic Press, Oakville, Ontario, Canada, 2019.

MOSAIC PRESS, Publishers

We acknowledge the Ontario Arts Council
for their support of our publishing program

MOSAIC PRESS
1252 Speers Road, Units 1 & 2
Oakville, Ontario L6L 5N9
phone: (905) 825-2130

info@mosaic-press.com

STELLA

CONTENTS

OLDEN TIME HOCKEY IN CANADA

Sometimes on a Saturday night, me and the two grandkids, we'll be watchin' *Hockey Night*, in the new multi-media extravaganza theatre thing we got in the basement. - Or maybe we're pickin' up a mid-week stream on the big screen. You understand what I'm sayin'? - Me and the boys, we're watchin' a game. Hockey.

So then comes on the between-periods Intermission. The two boys always get bored at that part. They start jerkin' around and wrestlin' and spillin' the popcorn. Me, I'm tryin' to see the First-Period Highlights, or listenin' to Don whats-is-name, because you might learn some important, insider technical stuff – but them two darned kids start friggin' around and makin' noise. -Hey, Grandpa, they always say, when's the Second Period coming on? Or: Hey Grandpa! Can we watch a dirty movie now?

They do that just to horse around. Because they know it gets under my skin when I'm tryin' to see the replays and the expert simulations, eh? They don't care nothing about the Science of the game. Also, they been brought up on the Toronto Maple Leafs – so naturally they don't take the game serious yet.

"You damned modern kids," I always say, "you don't appreciate how lucky you are. Here you are, surrounded by gigantic TVs, Eye-Phones, and Electronic War-Killing Games– and you can't never sit still for five minutes! Why, when I was a kid, we was lucky just to hear a game on an old crackly radio broadcast!"

And then the little buggers look at me strange. Because I realize of course – they don't know what I'm talkin' about. Kids today got no sense of History. You noticed that? So, just to keep them two shut up until the Second Period comes on, I tell them all about it. I mean, how it used to be. They don't teach them that stuff in school no more. They all grow up ignorant.

So anyways, I tell them all about olden-days hockey. Back in the day.

And this is what I say:

"Okay. Long, long ago, before the age of TV, any kids who wanted to see excellent hockey matches could not do so in the comfort of their own homes."

"The main reason was pretty simple: there weren't no TV sets."

"Okay, this is a funny idea, but nevertheless it is true. In them days, people only had old-fashioned radio sets, see? On Saturday night, they might maybe could *hear* a real NHLhockey game – but this is my point, they still could not see it. There was no picture."

"This was even before the time of black and white, remember."

"*Wow*! Was this even before the Rock Era, Grandpa?" says the one kid, pretty astonished.

"Certainly it was," I says. "What do you think I'm talkin' about?"

"Freak me out!" says the kid, whistling in admiration.

"What did kids *look* at then, Grandpa?" they says, the little smart-alecks.

"They didn't look at *nothing*," I says, irritated. "Aren't you payin' attention? I just said that. They had to *listen* – to the radio."

"On their headsets?"

" Headsets! They didn't have no earphones or headsets. Nor Eye-Phones neither."

They look at me definitely queer at that point, because they're pretty sure I'm pulling their leg now. I mean, not the part about TV

– the younger kid, Bradley, he says his teacher told them all about that. In school. When they were doing Current Events.

"Listen," I says, "you're getting me off the point. You kids, you can't listen for five minutes. You got no concentration."

But are they listening?

"Hey Grandpa," they says. "Take us out for a treat, eh?"

"Yeah, c'mon, Grandpa. You never take us nowheres, eh?"

"You damned kids," I says, "you're a pair of spoiled brats – you know that? What do you think – I'm made of money?"

"Aw c'mon! Don't be so cheap, Grandpa!"

"Yeah! What a tightwad, eh?"

"*Listen* you brats," I says. "I didn't say I was takin' you *nowheres*. I'm tryin' to tell you something important here. About the olden-days hockey."

"You been talking a *long* time, Grandpa!"

So we're ridin' in the car, eh? And them two, they're wrestlin' and punchin' each other in the back seat.

"Hey!" I says. "Watch the leather. Whaddya think this is, eh?"

"When you gonna trade in this junk-heap, Grandpa? This heap is falling apart!"

"*Heap*! Whaddya talking? This is a forty-seven-thousand-dollar automobile, two years old, for pete's sake!"

"Larry's Dad's got a new BMW, Grandpa," says the kid.

"Punch up mom's old *Megadeath* CD, Grandpa," says the other one.

But that's getting me off the point again. –Don't kids never pay no mind? I'm trying to explain them something important here. –*Hey*! I says. Can't you boys use your imaginations? Just think about how it would be like, what I'm telling you about. No TV's.

They both groan.

"You listen up, Bradley!"

Think about it. In the old days. Who'd ever get to see a real-live NHL game without a TV? Nobody. Unless you happened to live in Toronto, or in Montreal, Quebec – which had the only two NHL franchise teams in the entire Confederation, boys. – Sure, people who lived in Toronto or in Montreal Quebec, might sometimes get out to see a real, actual NHL game – but most people who lived in other parts of the country could not. They did not have TV's.

"Can't you drive faster, Grandpa?"

So what did most people do? -If they wanted to see excellent hockey, I mean, and there was no TV – what could they do?

The answer is simple: in those days, people used to go to the actual local ice-rink. They would go to the actual local arena where a game was being played and they would stand or sit there, watching the actual players playing the actual game. This is what people in those times meant by 'watching a hockey game.' "

Is this clear? You understand my point? They didn't have a television set, so they were hungry for any kind of hockey game they could see. So they would watch Pee-Wee games, Midget games, Juveniles and Juniors, and even old guys in the Seniors. They didn't care. Just so long as they could actually *see* something.

"Think about that one, boys," I says. "Can you imagine?"

"What do you mean, Grandpa?"

Well lookit: think about the considerable implications, boys – for example, there must've been thousands of people in this country who woulda figured the Toronto Maple Leafs would look, sorta, more or less like the fellas on the local Senior B team – and the Montreal Canadiens probably look pretty much the same as the Senior B fellas from the next burg down the road. – See my point? They wouldn't have no other true-to-life authentic picture in their heads to go by.

That's just the way it was. When people don't have TV sets, it's amazing what a false notion of reality they're going to get. Their imaginations just go wild and run up all kinds of crazy ideas. They get everything all wrong.

Just try to imagine what kind of idea somebody today might have of the NHL hockey, if he or she did not have a TV. Can you imagine?

That person would be so stupid, he could run his car right over Ron McLean or Sidney Crosby in the street, and not even know it was them.

I'm serious: he wouldn't even know it was them – unless, of course, they maybe yelled out something in terror just before he run them over. –He might recognize the voice from the radio, I mean. – But that's not the same thing. Besides, that's not my point, so let's not get off on a useless tangent.

Still photos, you might say? -The fella might have seen some photos of hockey guys in the weekend magazine or in the newspaper?

Now that's true enough. He might have seen some pictures laying around somewhere – so he'd sorta understand what some of the players and teams looked like.

Well ... you might have a bit of a point there ... I won't deny it. Or you could get a certain likeness to the real guys from hockey card pictures – but it's not the same, is it? Alright, so maybe then the fella wouldn't actually be so stupid as to run down Crosby or Ron McLean unknown in the street – he might have that much sense – but still, be fair: would he know what Crosby looked like in action?

Of course not. You see a still photo of a guy, and then you see him actually play hockey – it's hardly the same thing, is it? You wouldn't know if the guy was really good, or the worst bum in the league.

But that's not my point. My point is: an awful lot of people used to go to actual games – and why? - Because they got no choice.

Take some small town. Let's say it's Friday night. What're people gonna do for entertainment?

"They could go to the movies, Grandpa!"

"*Stupid*!" says the other guy, groaning. "*Now* he's gonna say they didn't have movies in the olden days, and we're gonna have to hear all about *that* for two hours – right, Grandpa?"

"Of *course,* they had movies!" I says. "What do you think we're talking here – the stone age?"

"Can we go home now, Grandpa?"

"Can I have another chocolate fudge sundae first, Grandpa?"

"Me too, Grandpa!"

"Another chocolate sundae? That's three each! What you think: money grows on trees?

"But we had to sit here for about *three hours*, Grandpa!"

Money, money, money. These kids, they don't want to understand the important facts of Canadian History, they just want to spend money. One other Saturday, we're in the Canadian Tire Store, lookin' at the new equipment.

"Grandpa! Grandpa! They got the new dyna-flex neuro-moulded skates!"

"Two hundred and ninety-nine-ninety-five!" I says. "I just got you new skates last September, didn't I?"

"That's the *old* model, Grandpa! C'mon, eh?"

"Look at those air-foil shin-pads, Grandpa! They got USB ports and a recharger for your cell phone!"

Shin-pads, I says. Now there's another thing you could learn from, boys – you take the olden days. Nobody had shin pads – kids used to use Eatons' Catalogues, then strap them on with cut-up inner-tube rubber from your sister's bicycle. For a hockey stick, some kid'd saw one out of a board, or pull a limb straight off a tree, boys – and your own great-grandfather, why, I remember him saying they'd use a piece of coal for a puck and play all day on a cow-pond! *Coal*, boys! That's the way it was in the old days, and you boys should know that.

"What's coal, Grandpa?"

These kids today don't even know what coal is.

I send them to the Hockey School in the summer.

"Listen," I says to the guy who owns the thing – this guy, he used to play in the pros, eh? You probably never heard of him, but he was up with the Bruins for a try-out once in the 90's, eh? "- Listen," I says, "the little fat one is a centreman, eh? And the big guy wants to play left wing." - I mean, the guy's got them both playing Defence, wastin' my time – what'm I payin' 1600 bucks a summer for – third stringers? Give me a break.

"Listen," I says, "this kid was an ace for his Atom team, John. – You know what I'm saying? The kid's a gunner."

"We'll give them a look," says John.

You can't get any satisfaction nowadays. They don't teach them the old fundamentals, like scoring goals. They got no tradition.

I'm speaking to Buddy Harris from the Leafs, eh? Buddy comes up for the day, as a guest-star goaltending instructor.

"Listen, *Buddy*," I says, "you see my kid here – the kid's a shooter, eh? They got him playing Defence. – Can you believe it? Listen – hey, Bradley, c'mere! Show Mr. Harris your stuff. – No, c'mon, Buddy, you got the pads on, just let the kid fire you a couple – no, c'mon, be a pal."

" So ... you seen that, Buddy?" I says. "Is that a wrist-shot, or what? Nobody knows how to shoot the old wrist-shot nowadays, what with all these slappers and two-pieced composite curved sticks, eh? Listen, I was telling my boys – you can back me up on this one – how in the old days, a guy would go out and practice the old wrist-shot by the hour. Up against the barn-door if he didn't have ice – or use a piece of coal if he didn't have a puck."

"What's coal?" says Buddy.

This guy's a 2-time Vezina Trophy winner. So the boys, they tell him all about what I said about the radio on Saturday night and how people didn't have TV's to see a game.

"I think your granddad's pulling your leg on that one, boys," says Buddy. "That's news to me."

After that, I can't get them to listen to anything. Sometimes we'll be sittin' watching the new Hockey Night In Canada – or we're pickin' up a game on the Sports Channel, and on will come Wayne Gretsky with his 'Wayne's World Hockey Legends' Series.

"Hey!" I says, yellin' up the stairs. "Hey, you boys! Hurry up down here! Look at this!"

They're cooking a frozen pizza in the microwave and wrestling and jerking around in the kitchen.

"Hurry up! You're missing all this!"

They come storming down the basement stairs, spilling cheese pizza and soft drinks.

"*You missed it!*" I says. "You blasted kids, you're never here when something important is on TV."

"What was it, Grandpa? A Terrorist Attack?"

"Listen," I says, "they just showed some old-time films. Exactly what I was tellin' you about, you smart alecks – old film about the old radio broadcasts by Foster Hewitt in the olden days. You know what I'm tellin' you? You could've seen the whole set-up. It was on Wayne Gretsky's Hockey Legends."

"Who's Foster Hewitt?" says the older one.

"Who's Wayne Gretsky?" says the other.

"You damned kids," I says, "you're totally ignorant – you know that? There it was, in black and white, right before your eyes, you could've seen just exactly how it was – and you guys are gone. You got the attention span of mayflies."

"What's mayflies, Grandpa?"

"*I knew you were going to say that!*"

It's the Christmas holidays, and we're in the plaza at the electronics store, checking out the new DVD's.

"Hey, Grandpa! Can we get a dirty movie?"

"Don't be disgusting, Bradley!"

"Larry Armstrong's father let's him look at dirty movies, Grandpa!"

"Larry Armstrong's father is a pervert."

"We're the only kids in Grade Five and Six not allowed to see dirty movies, Grandpa! All we get to do is hear old boring lectures about History!"

"Yeah! How are we supposed to *learn* anything! We don't get to do *anything*, Grandpa!"

That's another thing, I says, in the olden days, kids didn't just sit around the house like vegetables, watching dirty movies. They'd be outside, playing sports and makin' up games, in the good clean fresh air.

"What do you mean, Grandpa?"

"You mean kids used to play *outside*, Grandpa? In the *cold*?"

"Certainly!"

"In the *cold*, Grandpa?"

We go home. And I say: - Okay, boys, that's it – the last straw. It's about high time you darned boys learned a thing or two about toughness. – Go get the snow shovels out of the garage and then report around to the back-yard.

That's it. I get them two to tramp down all the snow in the backyard.

"We're going to build an ice-rink, boys," I says.

"An ice-rink!"

"But we haven't got a Zamboni machine, Grandpa!"

"Never mind that! Start tramping down all the snow in that dahlia bed. Flatten it all out. Get to work, Brian."

"My feet are getting wet, Grandpa!"

"Never mind that. Suck it up. Keep stomping!"

I keep them out there half of Saturday afternoon. Then half the next week I'm out there with the garden hose until it's finished and I'm soakin' wet and covered with ice. Next Saturday, I call them outa bed at 7:30 and tell them to get dressed and get their skates on.

"Aw, Grandpa! Are you serious?"

"It's *freezing* out, Grandpa!"

"You soft modern kids, it's only seventeen below, you're going to learn a thing or two. Report at the back door in ten minutes. I want hockey sticks and skates."

"Isn't this a bit harsh, dear?" says their grandmother, fluttering around and being anxious. "They're only little boys."

"They're getting totally soft and ignorant," I says. "Why in the olden days in the Christmas holidays, a kid would play hockey outdoors all day long - and still come back for more after supper. Certainly you remember that?"

"*We* always went to Florida for Christmas," she says.

"*Florida!*"

"You sound as though you're getting a sniffle, dear," she says mildly.

In ten minutes, the pair of them report to the back door, with their skates on and padded up in about sixteen woollen sweaters and toques and scarves and full snowsuits, and they're standing there pouting like a pair of bad-tempered Pillsbury dough-boys.

"Okay! Outside!"

"Aw Grandpa! Do we have to?"

"You just get out there and have fun, Bradley, and none of your lip!"

"What if somebody *sees* us, Grandpa!"

"Yeah! Everybody's going to think we're really *stupid!*"

"You just get out there and enjoy yourselves, you two, or else you're really going to be in *trouble!*"

"Boy, Grandpa, you're really *evil*!"

And they go out complaining and grumbling and trudge through the deep snow in their skates and waddle over the snow bank and onto the ice-rink.

"Look at that," I says, "they're just standing there - sulking."

There they are, standing in the centre of that little patch of ice, with their hockey sticks in their hands like limp noodles, and doing nothing.

"Hey!" I yells out the door. "Start *playing*!"

They start moving around a little bit, pushing at the puck with one hand and glaring at the house.

"Skate!" I hollers. "What are you — old women?"

I keep them out there 40 minutes. But after 10 minutes, Bradley's reclined backwards in a snowbank and is bloated out with sweaters and layers of clothes like the Michelin Man — and the other one is standing at the patio door, shivering and tapping his mittens on the glass like the lost man on some polar expedition.

"I don't think they're enjoying it, dear," says their grandmother, anxiously.

"Don't be silly," I says grimly. "They're having the time of their lives."

Listen, in the old days, hockey players had to have some real stamina and inner fortitude, boys. That was before the days of these big contracts and soft living. A fellow might work all day in the concrete block factory and then go out at night and score five goals. --Did you know that one guy might play an entire game without a line-change, Bradley?"

"I don't care, Grandpa!"

This is a modern-age kid. He's drinking cocoa and is wrapped up whimpering in a big eiderdown comforter in front of the blazing fireplace and he's got a red nose and is sniffling and coughing like some rheumatic.

They're both mad as wet hens.

"Are you our real Grandpa?"

"Now listen, you boys," I says, "I'm just trying to teach you something."

"Yeah, but you're *mean*!"

"We're gonna run away, Grandpa!"

"I want to go back to live with Mom!"

"Mom's not out of rehab yet, Brian, you know that."

Now listen, you boys, a little cold in the head is not going to hurt you. Why I remember in the old days we did not even have penicillin and ....

"*Grandma*! He's starting again!"

"I'm getting dizzy!" yells the other one, jumping up and staggering around feverishly. "Everything is spinning around!"

"I think I've got pneumonia, Grandma!"

After that, they won't listen to anything.

"He hates us, Grandma!"

"Yeah! What did we ever do to him?"

Every time I come into a room, they blench and exit, fast. They won't come near the TV room on Saturday night.

"Everett," says their grandmother anxiously, "shouldn't you try to make up? I'm getting worried. Do you think we should see a family counsellor?"

"Okay, boys," I says the next weekend. "Just to show there's no bad feelings, you can do anything you want to do today, my treat. So what do you want to do?"

They won't answer. They're both sitting in their room, cutting out colour-pictures from their rock magazines. They both scowl and look away.

"Come on, boys, I know you can hear me," I says, "so what do you want to do? You're making me feel like a dog."

They both look a little guilty at that.

"No, seriously, boys, I haven't been able to sleep for *days*, I felt that bad. I don't know how I can go on. I think this is the end, boys."

Their lips quiver a bit.

"Insomnia, boys, just because I felt so rotten about being mean to you two lads - believe me. I could get very sick. Now come on, aren't we still pals? So what's it to be? You name it. Anything you want to do. – Do you want me to break down on the floor and beg, boys?"

"Bradley and Brian," says their grandmother, her own lip quivering too, "- can't you see that your grand-dad is suffering? Can you be so cruel?"

Now they're both blubbering and snivelling like fools.

"Boys, boys," says their grandmother, bursting into tears. "Your grandpa takes you everywhere. You've got the best grandfather in Canada, boys, and all he wanted was that you should understand something about the olden days."

"I don't want you to grow up ignorant, boys," I says. "I just wanted to share a few memories of my own past with you. Maybe I was wrong – we were just *poor* kids, some of us lived down by the railway tracks, we had to use old sweater-sleeves for hockey stockings, that was all we could afford if our dad got sick and lost his job. – I just wanted you boys to know facts like that. Is that so cruel?"

"Now ...," I says. "I'm going out to the garage to tune up the snow blower. And while I'm gone, I want you two boys to think about all this."

"Your grandfather wants you to search your consciences, boys."

Twenty minutes later they come out to the garage.

"Grandpa!" blubbers Bradley, big tears streaming down his fat little cheeks. "We're rotten little selfish kids!"

"*Yeah*! We never think about *you*, grandpa! We just thought you were trying to torture us! We didn't understand!"

"I'm glad you've come to your senses, boys."

"Yeah! Listen! Grandma and Brian found this awesome old hockey place on the Internet, grandpa! It's still exactly like the old-fashioned days! Listen! They let you go right into this actual old arena and see the whole thing!"

"Well now, let's not ..."

"And it's not that far by car! We want to go, grandpa! Honest! It'll be just the way you like, grandpa! Just like when *you* were a kid!"

"Now, wait a minute here," I says, "there's no need to be too hasty. You boys don't have to go to extremes just to make it up to me. I thought maybe you might be more pleased to go to a video arcade, or perhaps ..."

"No! This time it's what *you* like, grandpa! We called up on the phone."

"You're not going to believe it, grandpa! They have *five* games all this afternoon! Five!"

"It'll be five times better than the NHL, grandpa!"

"You can't disappoint them, dear," whispers their grandmother.

Is this a nightmare?

Listen: two hours later, we're actually sitting in the stands of some rundown old tin-pot ice rink, out the back of beyond - a real old-fashioned ice-box. I didn't know they still built dumps like that. What is this, I says - the 19th century? Charles Dickens must've played here as a boy. This place is for orphans.

Brrr! I says. Jeez, what is this, the North Pole?

Listen, they don't bother putting any heating in these gimcrack places nowadays, did you know that? There's huge icicles hanging in the rafters of this barn, I kid you not. You can see people's breaths steaming up in the air, there's an arctic gale comes howling in the back door and through all the cracks in the tin walls.

I don't believe it. Didn't anybody ever hear about the 21st Century? This is mediaeval, I says. I'm sittin' there in my car-coat and gloves and my scarf pulled up around my ears and I'm shiverin' and shakin' like crazy. Also, you got to sit on some frozen unheated wood bench, which is like a cake of ice. Your whole rear-end is numb.

Eight bucks apiece for this horror-show? I says. This is some Industrial League. - Who are these guys?

"It's the G.M. Bulldogs versus the Northern Foundry Flyers, grandpa! says the kid. It's the game of the week."

I never seen such a bunch of hackers in my life, I says. – Look at that! That's a deliberate spear! That guy can't even skate. Who lets these guys loose in public?

"Wow! This is really *good,* grandpa!"

And the language! Who are these bums? These guys are animals. You wouldn't see bigger pot-bellies around the hot-stove league.

"You were right, grandpa! This is really awesome!"

"Yeah! You don't get this many fights on TV, grandpa!"

"Yeah! It's better than the dirty movie we saw at Larry Armstrong's, eh, Brian?"

I can't believe my eyes. It's like World War III.

"Listen, boys", I says, "probably you've had enough now – so, how about Burger King? I'm buyin'. The works."

"*Shhh*!" says the kid. "It's only the First Period."

"And there's still two more games, grandpa! After this one!"

"He broke his stick, grandpa! Right on that man's helmet!"

"Look, boys," I says, "you don't have to keep up the pretence for me. I know you're just tryin' to make up, so ..."

"*Shhh*!"

You can't get hot coffee in these dumps. Even if you're freezin' to death. – Did you know that? The stuff is lukewarm.

"Now people are fighting in the stands, grandpa!"

"*Wow*! Did you hear what that guy said, Brian? He said ..."

"Don't you *dare* repeat that, Bradley!"

Listen: what's this modern world coming to? A few hours later, I'm sitting at home in front of the blazing fireplace, shaking and shivering, and my nose is running, and I got a head like a balloon.

"You wouldn't believe how awesome it was grandma! Everybody was fighting! They had to call the police! And we were sitting right in the middle of it!"

"*Yeah*!"

"Yes, Bradley," says their grandmother. "But not now. Go get your grandfather another cup of hot cocoa."

"And bring the Neo-Citron and the aspirins," I croak.

"I think you have a fever, dear."

"Is this electric blanket turned right up?"

"And you can buy hot-dogs right in the arena, grandma! You don't even have to put them in the microwave yourself!"

"Yes, Bradley. It sounds perfect."

"I'm freezin' to death," I says. "I can't get warm."

"Just relax, dear."

"I could be dying of first grade pneumonia here."

"And grandma! Bradley and me want to go every week now! Grandpa was right! It's much better than TV."

"Yeah! It was just like the olden days hockey! Just like grandpa said!"

"I can't get warm," I says. "I'm never going to get warm again in my life. –Bradley, go get me a hot-water bottle."

"A what, grandpa?"

"A *hot-water bottle*! What's the matter - you deaf?"

"What's a hot-water bottle, grandpa?"

"We haven't had a hot-water bottle for years, dear. No one uses those any more."

"But at least Bradley and me understand all about olden-days hockey now, grandpa! You must be proud of us! Now we're not completely ignorant, eh?"

These kids today. They don't understand anything. But I try to break it to them gently.

"You damned pinhead kids!" I says. "You *still* got it all wrong!"

"But, grandpa ..."

"Listen," I says, with my teeth chattering. "What you boys witnessed today was *not* the way it used to be in the olden days. It wasn't that way at all."

"But, grandpa ..."

"Don't contradict me, Brian."

"But we asked another old guy, grandpa! While you were out sitting in the car, trying to get warm. That old man said that's *exactly* the way it used to be, grandpa, in olden-days hockey!"

"Yeah, grandpa!"

"And he was a really *old* guy, grandpa - even older than you. He was taking the tickets."

"In the *really olden* days, Bradley - if I can have your complete attention for a minute -- in the really olden days, everything was *not* like that. Everything was perfect. It was always happy and warm. Everybody was always smiling and cheerful. You did not have ..."

"But ...."

"I think you had to be there, dear," says their grandmother.

"But, grandma, the old man said ...."

"Don't be difficult, Bradley," I says, huddling up in my electric blanket.

"But, grandpa!"

"Don't argue with your grandfather, Bradley," says their grandmother. "Speak nicely to him. I think he's dying."

"But, grandma! The old man said ..."

"Don't they teach you *anything* in school nowadays, Bradley? Do you think you can go around being gullible and believing every strange old man you meet?"

"He might have been a *bad* man, Bradley," explains their grandmother gently. "That's what your grandfather means. Possibly that other old man was trying to lead you astray."

The kid's eyes pop open, astonished.

"Always listen to your grandfather, Bradley," says their grandmother. "It's the safest thing to do."

"*Wow!*" says the kid. "I didn't know that old guy was a *bad* man, grandpa!"

"You have much to learn, Bradley."

"And that bad old man was trying to lie to us, right, grandma? Is that what you think?"

"I think that's probably the case, Bradley. Probably that bad old man was trying to undermine your confidence in your grandfather, dear. – So ... so that he could lure you and Brian away."

"You mean ... you mean he was some kind of *pervert,* grandma?"

"Probably so, Bradley. Hockey arenas are well-known resorts for that sort of person. Nowadays, I mean."

"Wow! We don't want to go *there* any more, grandpa!"

"Yeah! We better stay home and watch TV from now on, grandpa."

"That's probably wise, boys."

"But how did that old man get so *bad*, grandpa? He seemed such a nice old guy."

"Probably from watching dirty movies, Bradley."

"*Wow!*"

"I think that's enough now, boys," says their grandmother. "Your grandfather needs to rest now. He's had a hard day."

"Okay, grandma."

But they both hang around the door a minute.

"Grandpa? We really learned something today.:

"I'm glad, Brian. But I can't talk now. I think I've got pneumonia."

"Before today, we really thought you were pulling our leg."

"Before today, you were very ignorant, Brian."

"You see, boys," says their grandmother kindly, ushering them to the door, "many people believe that children who grow up only on TV and have no sense of Canadian history will believe anything that anybody tells them - these children may be gullible and easily deceived. This is the lesson that your grandfather was trying to teach you, Brian. – Do you understand now?"

The kid considers this thoughtfully.

"What's 'gullible', grandma?"

You see? Kids today don't learn *anything*.

***

THE PETE McKEEN STORY

As Told To

AL GUFFUM

Veteran Sports Writer

Moose River Angler

DEDICATED

To Kids Everywhere

Who Have a Dream

BEGINNINGS

As the temperature dropped to minus 50 degrees, bitter arctic winds blew real fierce in the great north, dumping another 18 feet of snow over the vast, lone forests and small towns of remote Northern Ontario, where young Pete McKeen lived.

But young Pete McKeen did not mind snow. At the crack of dawn, young Pete was out the door of his house and shovelling like mad. How the snow flew! For Pete had learned that snow-shovelling was one of the best ways a healthy young boy could build up strong arms and lungs and a healthy cardio-vascular system and get to be a professional hockey player and score twenty goals a season and earn over 3500 dollars per year, cash money - not counting clothing-allowance bonuses.

This is how it all started.

"Ma, I'm going to be a hockey player when I grow up," Pete had said one Saturday night, as his ear was glued to his crystal radio set, to hear Foster Hewitt and Hockey Night in Canada, on the distant CBC.

"Better get out and shovel the path to town again then," said Pete's mother.

"Why's that?" asked Pete.

"That's how professional hockey players all get started," claimed Pete's mother. "Helps both strength and stick control. So get cracking. And watch out for the wolves."

"*Wow!*" said Pete. "Is that how Max Bentley got started?" (For Max was his boyhood idol.)

"You bet," said Mrs. McKeen.

After that, you couldn't keep young Pete away from a snow shovel – unless there was a shinny game going on down at the lake.

"I could be a hockey player for sure now," said Pete. "Look at these biceps!"

"Why not become a doctor instead," said his mother. "That way, if things don't work out ..."

But Pete knew in his heart that, one day, a pro hockey scout from a famous big-city team would be coming to his town; and so every morning after shovelling the half-mile to town, Pete grabbed the blades, shouldered the old trusty one-piece lumber, and hustled down to the big ice surface of Wiggins Lake, where an impromptu pick-up game of real old-time shinny was sure to be going on, day or night.

That was because the Northern Ontario town of Wiggins Lake was, in the old days, the premier, number-one, ice-hockey-hotbed of Ontario – where no self-respecting male or female did *anything* all day – or half the night – except play shinny.

"Never let school or a job get in the way of a good shinny game," advised the town elders.

The same message was preached every Sunday, at Wiggins Lake Presbyterian Church.

"We thank Thee, O Lord," the Reverend Jock McCabe always intoned, in his closing Sunday morning benediction, "as we go forth today to play hockey. - And God bless the Toronto Maple Leafs, as they too go forth, this week's NHL schedule, to slay the Detroit Red Wings and chastise the wicked Chicago Black Hawks. Amen. Go in Peace."

"Rev. McCabe," little Pete once asked, when 5-year-old Petey first started Sunday School, "will there still be hockey, if little children are good and go to Heaven?"

"And does not the Book say that, in God's heavenly realm, all things will be perfected?"

"It does."

"Well then."

Pete pondered this and then said:

"But does that mean that Americans will finally learn how to play hockey too?"

"I doubt many of them will be there," said the Reverend, with a frown.

This was because the Reverend McCabe had once done 2 seasons, semi-pro, with the old Hershey Bears, before getting drafted into religion. But he had not enjoyed his residence south of the border.

"The beer," he said. "Evil. You wouldn't believe it."

So hockey was a deep, deep passion in Pete's part of the north woods. And what incredible hockey talent resided there, in that one remote town! Some people claimed that in one morning alone, more amazing, genius-like, shinny talent could have been recruited out of Wiggins Lake, in those first post-war days, than from any other town, hamlet, or incorporated village in the rest of the province! - If only the big-city hockey scouts had not been so stunningly blind!

In Wiggins Lake, all the grizzly old men, keen-eyed young lads, and every clumsily growing boy *adored* hockey – and the girls and advanced young married women were just as hockey-mad– even sneaking prematurely out of their pews during a Sunday morning service, before the Reverend Jock had completed his benediction - so they wouldn't miss first dibs and choosing-up-sides for the big all-community shinny game, the one that always took place on Wiggins Lake right after Sunday church.

"*Ladies, ladies!* I said: *'Go in Peace!'*" protested the Reverend McCabe. "Let the Minister get out the door first, dammit!"

For the Reverend Jock McCabe had to run all the way up the hill to the Manse, to grab his own skates and stick – while most of his Congregation lived in houses right by Wiggins Lake itself, so didn't have nearly so far to go.

But *hockey, hockey, hockey*! That was all that anybody who was balanced and respectable ever thought about in Wiggins Lake, on *any* day of a winter week!

Of course, in those early days after the war, after the shutdown of the iron mine, and after the closure of the German POW internment camp out near Muskrat Falls, there was really nothing much else to do in winter. - Except for the ice-fishing, of course. But ice-fishing and shinny *just cannot compare*, as every sane person knows.

"Well, I don't know," worried Pete's mother, a little skeptically. "A man can at least feed his family with the ice-fishing, Peter. But you can't eat hockey pucks."

"But just look at this, ma!" countered Pete excitedly, showing his mum an old edition of *The Hockey News*, which was flown in by daring bush pilots, every second month!

"Just see here, ma! See the picture? – it says Rocket Richard gets paid 35 bucks, cash money, every week! *Just for playing hockey!* Plus, he gets a bonus summer job, delivering Molson beer! - And look at Gordie Howe! During his off-season, *he* gets guaranteed 42.5-hours summer work, flat-rate, at the cement block plant back home in Saskatchewan! - It's in his contract! – Ma! Nobody earns big money like that around here!"

"Well …," said Pete's mother (for those were pretty difficult economic numbers to argue with), "yes, but, those two particular young men are *very* big stars, remember."

"Yes, sure, but …"

"Nonetheless, I still feel you should have a back-up plan and *also* become a medical doctor, Peter …"

But Pete was not listening. Instead he was off again, furiously shovelling his way down to the town and the lake, for another shinny game – and for another season of developing his all-important hockey skills.

-And all that dedication paid off, kids. By the time Pete was 17, he had developed into one of the best young prospects in Northwestern Ontario! Dandy Pete, he was nicknamed. He had all the tools. - So all he had to do now, was to sit back and wait until that big-time professional NHL hockey-scout came to town!

But still Pete's mother fretted about his future.

"I do hope you're also taking care of your schooling, Peter," she said, wanly.

Guiltily, Pete looked at his mother. For like all good, young Canadian hockey players, he loved his mom – and didn't want to disappoint her. Not after all the tender support she had given him growing up – always seeing that his old CCM tube skates were sharp and polished; washing his long johns and sweaty hockey socks by hand in the old tin tub and wash-board in the kitchen; ensuring that he always had a new snow shovel for Christmas, even when money was short.

"Don't worry, ma," said Pete. "I'll stick in school and get my high school, before I go off to make pots of cash in the Pros."

And Pete was as good as his word – for Pete was a very smart boy, who did well in every subject in school. In fact, when high-school graduation arrived, Pete was at the very top of his class *in everything*– even, for the first time in recent history, topping the astonishing academic marks of Jo-Annie Alcott, "The Girl Brain" of Wiggins Lake Secondary School. And because of that academic achievement, Pete even won a scholarship interview and a chance for full board and tuition to a big American college!

Pete's mother was so proud!

A college recruiter came to town, for Pete's initial interview.

"*Whoa!*" said Pete, leafing through the college brochure and prospectus. "Your college doesn't even have a *hockey team?*"

"A *what?*"

"Don't pass up this chance, Peter. You'd probably break my heart right in two," said Pete's mom that night, putting some mild pressure on her boy.

"But they don't even have a hockey team, ma," said Pete. "What the point of a college degree, if there's no hockey?"

For Pete was a Canadian boy – and always kept things in perspective, when considering his future education.

"But it's a *medical* scholarship, Peter! Those things don't grow on trees."

"I know, ma," said Pete, reluctantly. "But why would a big-time professional hockey-scout visit a place that doesn't even have a hockey team? They wouldn't."

Mrs. McKeen could see the logic of this. But still, her motherly heart was set upon her boy becoming a medical doctor.

"At least go for the second interview," urged Pete's mother. "They've invited you to come down personally to see their nice college – and they've sent your ticket. They really seem to want you. Where's the harm?"

In the end, Pete decided he would go for the second interview and take the expense-paid campus tour. Because he did not want to disappoint his mom.

"You're a polite, loving Canadian boy, Peter," said Pete's mother. "That's why everybody thinks you'd make such a good doctor," she added. "*-Not that I'm trying to influence you!*"

That night in his room, Pete looked again at the college brochure and the railroad voucher, out of Winnipeg, that he had received by bush-pilot delivery. This college looked like a very intellectual institution. There seemed to be a lot of girls. And the place seemed to be loaded with money.

"How come these American colleges have so much spare cash, ma?" Pete asked in puzzlement.

"Well," said Mrs. McKeen, "it seems they get huge donations from their rich alumni – because of their football teams. It's what people mostly study at college down there. Even their pert young ladies."

"*Football!*" exclaimed Pete in utter astonishment.

"Yes."

"But how can that be?"

It was some weeks later that Pete got his confirmation and travel schedule from the rich American college, telling Pete when exactly he was to journey south, for his campus tour and final interview.

"*Oh, bloody hell!*" Pete cried out when he read the letter.

"Don't swear that dirty, dirty word, Peter! '*Hell*' is not a nice thing to say!"

"Sorry."

"Nice people don't want to hear about *that*, Peter."

"No, sorry, ma."

"But what's the matter? - Oh dear, don't tell me they've changed their minds about the scholarship?"

"No. But look at this travel schedule!"

"Yes?"

"I'd have to leave before the 1st of March, latest, to get there on time! Last dog-sled south, before the melt!"

"Well?"

"*But ma*! That's the night of the Junior C Trophy Final! And my team is in it! All the guys and me! - Plus, it's the inauguration of the new Town Arena!"

For during the past summer, the town council of Wiggins Lake had acquired, cheap, two unwanted RCAF-surplus, rusty, corrugated Quonset aircraft hangers, from the old, de-commissioned wartime flying base at Chipmunk Landing; and the local men had welded and re-bolted them together to make a neat, new Wiggins Lake Town Arena. – The Reeve and Council got the war-surplus hangers for practically nothing, because it was Federal Election Year.

"*But ma!* All the guys *need* me there! I'm second assistant Captain!"

"I am very sorry, Peter. You will just have to miss it."

"*Ma!*"

"Peter, I am not going to argue with you. You will just have to miss your precious hockey game, this one time. This interview is far, far too important for your future."

"Ma! I'm top scorer!"

"*Pe-ter McKeen!*" said Pete's mother sternly, putting on her absolutely-no-nonsense face, "I am putting my foot down! *You-are-going-to-this-college-interview*, young man – and no more debate about it!"

"But …"

"*Silence!*"

Well, as everybody knows, decent young Canadian hockey players always obey their moms. And so, in the end, Pete did as he was told –reluctantly travelling south for his American college interview, skipping and missing the big chance to be centre-man on the first line of the Wiggins Lake Warriors, in the Big Junior C Final *and* Arena Inauguration. Pete did not play. He missed that hugely important game. He chose to go to the college interview instead. Just because of a stupid all-paid medical scholarship.

"Why *inna hell* would anybody want t'do *that*?" all the grizzled old men sitting at the counter of Elmer's *Sprucewood Café* asked themselves, pushing back the ear-flaps of their plaid wool caps and scratching their heads.

"Kids today, eh? College."

In the end, after his interview, Pete wasn't even able to get back to Wiggins Lake for an extra two weeks - the lake ice having broken up early that year, so that even the queen of the dare-devil bush pilots, Myrtle "Dolly" McCabe, (the Reverend Jock's grandma), could no longer wing it in on skis, with her aging pink Norseman - not until the broken lake ice cleared off and the summer landing floats were bolted on. Nor could the seasonal gravel road to Wiggins Lake be re-opened by the provincial government until after the Spring porcupine migrations - Pete finally hitching a ride home in a fuel-supply tanker truck from Big Moose River.

"Ma! I'm back!"

"*Peter, darling! How did it go?*" Mrs. McKeen eagerly shouted, rushing in from chopping at the wood pile out back. "*Tell me, tell me! What happened?*"

"Got the thing, I guess."

"*You got your scholarship!*"

"Seems."

"*Oh, Peter! I'm so proud of you! You're going to be a medical doctor!*"

"Seems, eh?"

"Oh, Peter. What a wonderful, *wonderful* achievement!"

"Not bad. Can't complain. - Could be worse."

"You're not ecstatic?"

"Probably. – Who won the Final?"

"What?"

"The Muskrat Trophy."

"Oh … well, your team did. 4-2."

"*What? We finally won the Final?*" Pete McKeen wailed. "*- And I wasn't even there?*"

"Peter, it was only a hockey game."

Pete looked at his mom in utter disbelief. Who *was* this woman?

That afternoon, Pete went down to town, to the dingy old Sprucewood Café, where he and the team usually hung out after school, to play the pinball machine and look at girls.

"Pete the Man! You'll never guess!"

"Yeah, yeah," Pete said mournfully. "I heard."

"No, no! Not that. The big deal is … *they* were here! Three of those guys!"

"Who?"

"Real, big-time, NHL hockey scouts! Come all the way up from *Tra-na*! - No, seriously, *they were*! Actually in Wiggins Lake!"

Pete was so shocked that he dropped his orange pop right on the floor.

"Oh … no! - Oh …no, no, no!"

Three actual, big-time NHL Professional Hockey Scouts finally come to his home town! Truly, for real, arrived to check out the talent in Wiggins Lake! -Just as Pete had always dreamed? – And Pete had been away down south, just to get some stupid all-paid medical scholarship at some stupid American college?

Well, that is why that particular, grey, early springtime morning in Wiggins Lake was one of the most grey, tragical springtime mornings in the entire history of the community – at least for Pete McKeen.

A whole top line of NHL talent hunters finally, actually, for real, had come to town. And Pete McKeen had missed the one chance in his lifetime to get himself professionally scouted, discovered, and picked up by a real-life NHL team! And of course, eventually, *to win the Stanley Cup*!

But now, young Peter McKeen could never make 35 bucks a week, plus paid bus rides and meals, nor become famous and talked about on the radio by Foster Hewitt on Saturday Night!

And worse still, *he would never win the Stanley Cup*! Nor have his own individual "Pete McKeen, Number 11" hockey card in an O'Pee'Chee 5-card, NHL hockey team chewing gum pack, 10 cents! - Both of which ambitions had been Pete's whole secret plan and purpose of his mortal existence since he was 8 years old – *but especially winning the Stanley Cup! Every Canadian boy and girl's true destiny!*

For why else had God so strategically and geographically placed Canada, on the Final Day of Creation, exactly and precisely in the Great Frozen North – rather than in, say, Miami, Florida or frost-free Las Vegas? - What else could God have intended, but that every Canadian boy or girl, in such a favoured environment, would grow up to yearn for nothing else in life, but *playing hockey and winning the Stanley Cup?*

But now, for Peter McKeen, all that was lost! Forever!

"And guess what else!" said the boys down at the Sprucewood Café. "Fats Ferris got signed to a try-out - with the Toronto Marlies - next Fall!"

- *Ernie Ferris!? That* guy? A guy, who couldn't hit a hockey net with a puck the size of a Science Council of Canada weather balloon? *He* got selected? While Pete McKeen, the dandiest young hockey talent in all Wiggins Lake– he didn't even get a look-in?

Well, no more can be said about it. It was all just too tragical for words. So close, yet so far! -But then, as everybody knows, hockey is a game of inches. Miss by an inch, and you might as well miss by two inches, as Max Bentley once said.

For, when we come right down to it – right down to the brass Tackaberrys of the matter, as Max Bentley's brother, Doug, also liked to put it – NHL hockey scouting is hardly an exact science. It's more, entirely, a blind, drunken statistical crap shoot, as Albert Einstein also once said to Bill Bentley, Max and Doug's dad. Pure Luck of Chance, Albert said, and that's the scientific reason why only three of Bill Bentley's six Saskatchewan boys got signed to the NHL – and exactly three didn't.

"See," said Bill Bentley, "that's precisely 50-50. Albert says he could have predicted those odds, any day."

However, young Pete McKeen did feel a *little* better after he had read this objective scientific explanation of hockey scouting, in an old copy of *The Hockey News.* That was in an interview with Albert Einstein himself, when Albert was explaining his own hockey fantasy pool strategies. Albert again laid it out that exactly 50% of brilliant, talented, young Canadian hockey players *never had a statistical chance in the first place*! Mathematical certainty.

And that's why, in all the long, long years of recorded Canadian hockey history —since about 1897 or so - there have been thousands and thousands and even *thousands* of great, locally outstanding small-town hockey stars – guys who have potted a hat trick in a Pee Wee contest, or had four assists in the Bantam Final —but were still criminally overlooked by the big-league scouts.

All that shinny talent never spotted! All those brilliant small-town players never to win the Stanley Cup! I know I was one. That's why I had to become a sports writer. -Although I did actually *see* the Stanley Cup once, in the sweaty dressing room of the Toronto Maple Leafs, after their 1948 victory.

"Don't touch that, Guffum," ordered Syl Apps, picking up his hockey stick.

In fact, in small-town Canada, coast-to coast, what guy have you ever known who laced up the blades and scored a breakaway short-hander in the third period of the Midget Final – who still didn't end up getting overlooked by the scouts? - And having instead to make his living at the Ford Motor Plant, or as an Insurance Agent, or as an obscure Brain Surgeon or Supreme Court Judge, instead of rightfully stepping out onto NHL centre ice on a Saturday Night at Maple Leaf Gardens, or taking his warm-up with the Habs at the old Montreal Forum?

Every one of those thousands and thousands of overlooked lads *should have rightfully been in the NHL and winning a Stanley Cup.* But why didn't they? Just because of bad scouting.

So, okay, to be fair, maybe a few guys got missed for other reasons – maybe because a young guy was unfortunately tucked up in bed at home with the measles, *that one single day* when a Big-

Time Scout came to town; or just because another young guy was illegally night-fishing with a car-headlight with his uncle, instead of showing up for some match; or when some incredible, young hero was stuck at a shotgun wedding and reception – or when, like Pete McKeen, his mother had made him go to a college medical scholarship interview that day, in the U.S.A., instead of taking care of more important business at home.

For Pete, it was all just so unfair.

"Well, young Peter McKeen, I commiserate for your bleak and life-ravaging disappointment," consoled the Reverend McCabe the next Sunday morning, giving young Pete spiritual comfort at the church door. "Especially as no professional hockey scouts aren't never likely to ever again pass through our remote neck of the woods soon, or perhaps ever again in your entire, now-failed lifetime."

"But in our mortal existence, young Peter," the Reverend continued with a consoling homily, "we must all accept the higher laws of chance, as the Good Book tells us. - For our earthly fates – well, more yours than mine – so often bring in a tragic passage. Look at the terrible season the Leafs had in '46. - But your mother tells us that you might be a medical doctor now. That could be some small comfort to somebody. So cheer up. I'll be up at the manse after lunch and the hockey game, if you need any more spiritual counselling. 3-4 p.m."

Well, even though Pete's entire life was now utterly ruined and pointless, it was still far from over. For Pete was still a young man, with years and years of regret ahead of him. So Pete now had no real choice in life, but to become a medical doctor. - So Pete *did* go on to medical school – and he did become a doctor. Over time, in fact, a very celebrated medical doctor and research specialist. In fact, Dr. Peter later became so respected, that he was invited to join the distinguished medical faculty of McGill University in far-off Montreal, where in just a few more years, Pete had become internationally famed as the world's leading physiological authority on undefined lower-body hockey injuries. And a little later still in time, he was endowed with his own research laboratory. (*The McKeen Institute for the Advanced Study of Mysterious Shinny Ailments*), where Pete and his research assistants pioneered cutting-edge, revolutionary investigations, as reported in his ground-breaking, comprehensive study, *Physio-Neurological-Electro-Chemical-Sub-Particle-Substrates of Hockey Groin and Hamstring Injuries.* (McKeen. 1995) – the greatest treatise on lower-body research ever undertaken in the modern Canadian Shinny Sciences.

That revolutionary scientific research, of course, is the reason why Pete won the Nobel Prize for Sports Medicine, in 1997.

"Awarded for Brilliant Scientific/Medical Advancement of Our Knowledge of the Substrates of Really Unpleasant Bodily Occurrences in Canadian Shinny-Playing, As Particularly Expressed in Hamstring and Groin Injuries in the National Hockey League During Stanley Cup Playoff Runs," said the citation from the Nobel Prize Committee, when Pete had to go to Stockholm to get his award.

But unfortunately, this overseas trip also involved Pete, again, in needlessly and frustratingly missing a really big game he was scheduled to play, with his buddies on his Old Timers team, the Montreal West Wobblies, in the C Division Final of the renowned, annual Pointe Claire Old Timers Tournament. Pete did not get to play. He missed another big game of his life! Just because his mom made him go to Stockholm.

"Again!" exclaimed Pete. *"God!"*

"Peter McKeen!" said Pete's mother, *"You-are-going-to-this-Nobel-Prize-Award-Ceremony,* young man! – and no more debate about it!"

"But ma! I'm centre on the checking line!"

"Silence!"

So Pete ended up going to Stockholm to get his stupid Nobel award, even though it meant missing his Old-timers game. - For good Canadian hockey players always obey their moms, even when they are 58 years old.

Nonetheless, missing that Old-timers game was just one more bitter shinny disappointment for Peter McKeen. For his beloved Montreal West Wobblies won the Final in their Division, 15-12, and all the other guys got a beer mug to take home and put on the mantlepiece. *Except Pete!* For, again, Pete wasn't even there! – Just because he had to fly to Stockholm, to get some stupid Nobel Prize.

But Pete's mom was so proud. So too was Pete's wife, the highly regarded Neuroscientist, Jo-Annie Alcott-McKeen. (*Meta-Analysis of Adverse Neurological Effects on Test-Subjects Playing Hockey Wearing Woollen Toques, Instead of Plastic Hockey Helmets.* [Alcott-McKeen, 1988])

Wiggins Lake was also proud. After the Nobel Prize Ceremony in Stockholm, a fine fibreglass statue of Pete McKeen, was commissioned in Wiggins Lake, to stand forever in the parking lot of the Wiggins Lake Town Arena – where Pete's adventure had all begun, so many years before.

And there it still stands, a fibreglass-sculpted young Pete McKeen gazing in visionary fashion out over the snowy surface of Wiggins Lake – equipped with replica, vintage CCM tube skates and his trade-mark snow shovel. All molded and finished artistically by the famous *WiggyLake Fibreglass Canoe Co-operative.* And with a plaque attached, reading *"Pride of Wiggins Lake, and Area."*

The news of the awarding of the Nobel, of course, had come as an entirely unexpected, surprise to Pete – for despite his professional fame, Pete McKeen always remained a modest, self-deprecating, prudently restrained small-town Ontario boy, as all decent Canadian hockey players are, coast-to-coast - and even more so above the Arctic Circle, where until recently hockey had to be played even more carefully, on shifting sea-ice, so often suicidal due to ice fissures and polar bears.

Pete first learned of his Nobel award one Thursday night, at his family home in Montreal West, while he was watching the Habs getting mercilessly drubbed 7-2 by the Boston Bruins, in the first round of the Stanley Cup Playoffs.

As a matter of fact, and for the record, Pete actually first learned of his Nobel award from *me*, Al Guffum, as I had just got an early scoop from my old pal, Bjorn Born, Swedish pro from the 80's Oilers. You may remember the guy, had to retire early because of an undisclosed upper body injury. Now on the Nobel Prize Selection Committee. I ghost-wrote the bio for Bjorn's hockey card.

"The Nobel?" whispered Bjornie over the phone, carefully lowering his voice. "McKeen, of course. Who else? Don't tell anybody where you got this, Guffum."

"I owe you, pal."

I got right on the blower to Montreal. Fortunately, it was between periods, and Pete came right on the line, as he was down in the kitchen getting cookies and milk."

"*Petey boy*! - Al Guffum here! *Moose River Angler*! Remember me? - Just a quick tinkle to tell you - you're winning the Nobel Prize. But don't tell the wife. It's still secret."

"Okay," said Pete. "So how're you doin', Al? Long time no see. How's the wife and kids?"

"Pete? Could you give us a comment for *The Angler*?"

"On what, Al?"

"On this Nobel thing."

"Well…"

"Just a word or two? Can you describe what you're feeling right now?"

"Well …"

"Just a few emotional reactions? Readers love that stuff."

"Well, I guess I'd probably say … not bad … can't complain … could be worse. - Is that enough?"

"So then I can quote that you're ecstatic? Over the moon? – Or is that going too far?"

"Well …"

"Overwhelmed? – Fulfillment of a life-long dream?"

"Don't put this thing out of all rational proportion, Al," cautioned Pete McKeen. "It's just a Nobel Prize. It's not the Stanley Cup."

****

HOCKEY NIGHT IN THE ROUGH TOWNS

FOREWORD

BY

PLUG MACFARLAND

Former Defensive Standout North Dunoon Essos

Boys, now that I'm in the twilight part of my own hockey career, a lot of people ask me: Plug, what was the greatest hockey game you ever seen?

Now you might think that'd be a tough question for a man who's played, man and boy, in half the great shinny barns in Southwestern Ontario in his time, and nearly had a look-in with the Chatham Maroons in 1956. Frankly, I probably played in, coached, and seen hundreds of outstanding excellent hockey matches, whether you're talkin' Midget C, Juvenile or Junior D, or even the old Senior B loop down in Middlesex County. I seen play-off matches from Walkerton to Wingham, from Wiarton to West Lorne, make your hair stand on end. I seen sterling classics, the likes of which will never again be seen again - and one time when we come up underdogs to the Counties Semi-Finals, I seen a Senior B team from Strathroy, Ontario, could knock the socks off half the teams in the NHL today.

So I seen some dandy hockey in my time.

But I'll tell ya frankly: when some green kid comes over to me in the old Beverage Room of The Queens Hotel and says: 'Plug, what's the greatest hockey game you ever seen?' I got no trouble with that answer. I just look that kid straight in the eye.

"Son," I says, "I seen hundreds of excellent hockey matches in my time - but I'll tell ya fair, the most outstanding hockey game I ever seen in my entire lifetime has got to be the great Silver Flyer-Lumberman Final of 1962. That was the game of the century, boys, no word of a lie.

And then that damned pup of a kid, he's probably gonna roll his eyes and say: "Silver Flyers and Lumbermen? Whaddya *talkin*? I never heard of *neither* of them two teams!'

Well boys ... what can you do? Young pups today sure as hell don't know much about nothin' – and they sure as hell don't know much about hockey neither.

Sometimes it makes you feel like givin' up. There you'd got one of the very finest exhibitions of championship ice-hockey ever put forward in this god-forsaken country, and who remembers? You'd figure somebody woulda kept a record of the damned thing.

Well boys, enough is enough.

So finally here it is. Here's some other guy to tell about it.

So listen up:

Hockey Night in The Rough Towns

1.

I guess everybody in the world remembers the big final game of the Purina Cup, which was played out over in North Dunoon Township in 1962.

That was the night, over in the town of Mt. Pocock, when Gough's Lumber and Building Supply whipped the South Middlesex Silver Flyers 7-6 in overtime, thereby bringing down the roof of the Lorne Pocock Memorial Arena and Community Centre.

We're talking Sudden Death. And at the sight of that final, flashing, red goal light, an ungodly howl of triumph and revenge went up in the hometown rink. Hats and buckle-galoshes covered the ice – and Police Chief Ray Pocock had to call up his constable out of bed, to come down and help handle the crowd control. The losers were hooted off the ice mercilessly - because everybody knew the victory was a sweet vindication of the rough-town style.

"Well boys," Plug MacFarland observed to the Assembled Press in the victors' jubilant dressing-room, "I imagine all them boy figure-skaters know where to shove their dipsy-doodle now, eh? - It might look fancy, but it don't win no ball games around here."

And Plug was right. Silver-bladed hockey had been brought to its knees. And a gloating spirit of revenge was in the air.

How to explain?

One hard fact: Bad blood. The local Press was to blame. Because the very weekend before the big final game, the treacherous Gordon "Crunch" Routledge, county sports stringer for the great *London Free Press,* had stirred up the rural hornet's nest, blatantly coming out in the authority of newsprint to cast a cowardly, vile, and provocative libel upon the town honour of all loyal Mt. Pocockians:

Stick-handlin' around the old inter-county loop previous to this season's puck sched. (young Crunch had written in his much-admired rural hockey column, BEHIND THE TWINES) *the ol' scribbler must have been skating with his head down ... because now, as the local gladiators head for the wire, the old Cruncher has got to admit that this season he took some heavy hits right smack in the old prognosis ... Worst jolt came from the S.M. Silver Flyers club which he tagged to miss the money again this outing! ... Well the ol' ink-slinger blew that one, afficiandos!!!! The Fancy Flyers burst quick from the back of the pack and sculled away ... a flashy squad whose nifty playmaking and heads-up razzle-dazzle quickly boosted them to the top rung of local shinnydom, with an annum tally of 12 big W's and only 3 L's, as they head into the decider against the Mt. Pocock Ploughboys.*

... Well, with that kind of peppy track-record, Mt. Pocock beware!!!!! Statistics and classy form got to count in this one, and the ol' C has gotta slate the Fancy-F's for the Purina Cup and All the Marbles, no two ways!!! Unlike some of the hackers in these parts who call themselves hockey players (!!!!!), the Flyers stick to a clean game of skill and thoroughbred form. They got all the moves, led by the zippy sharp-shooting of the great Tommy Brookes (age 13) nailing down the centre slot, flanked on one side by the stylish Smithers at the starboard, and also the league's leading marksman B. Poole manning the port. Likewise, the Flyers are royally served in the rearguard, having durable defensive duos in the Grant-Brown combo, and in the match-up that sees Macdonald siding big Tidham at the blueline. ... But between the pipes, says some cynic? Well, scoffers, Tight Tooley didn't get his handle

for nothing. - He's tough in the twines, with a goals-against av. of just 5.2 to top the local circuit.

... The Big One is Friday at Mt. Pocock' country H.Q., but home ice advantage should be no advantage to the ploughboys. They're bush-whackers, fans. Strictly no finesse. Should be a walkaway for the clean-skating Flyers.

Fortunately for Crunch, the harness-racing season was coming up, and a few months later he was able to salvage his professional reputation in his summer column, AT THE WIRE - which was only fair, because Routledge was no natural-born fool, merely a pundit who put his money on Form and Training.

"See," says Plug MacFarland, "in them days, you still had your old traditionalists who understood the finer points of the game, as it used to be played in its natural way. – And then you had your narrow-minded young punks, who didn't know nothing. Them guys would make you sick, always yapping about cleanness and averages and all that kinda stuff. Jeez, you'd think the game was being played by a bunch of arithmetic teachers, to hear them guys talk!"

And as for Routledge's cowardly insinuation that the Mt. Pocockians were bush-whackers, … well, the afternoon when the offending copy of the great *London Free Press* reached the Victory Wet Bar of the Mt. Pocock Legion Hall, half the standing members immediately threw off their coats and testified that the post-war world was getting too damned sissy for its own good.

"See," explains Plug MacFarland, who has studied the art of ice-hockey man and boy, "there's two kinds of people in this world: there's the Nurse Nancies like that Routledge dummy; and then there's the rugged, manly individualists, let's call it, like myself. – Now speaking personally from my own point of view, I got nothing against those people – but you got to admit they lost the old élang vital (like they say up in Rouen-Noranda) and misery likes company. So the first thing these anemic boobs do, is they want everything planned out and organized, like a buncha robots. I mean, they hand out enough rules and tips and playing patterns to give a elephant a migraine. And once you let that stuff get started, you can't hardly move without some lawyer readin' you the book. There goes all the fun. Jeez, you can't hardly tell one team from the next, and pretty soon even the players on your own team are all wearin' matching uniforms," says Plug sourly, "like they was all the same guy."

Tough talk. And late at night, when the mournful echoes of Last Round have sounded in the Victory Wet Bar of the Mt. Pocock Legion Hall, when the tinkle of glasses is stilled, and when the very last *Theee ...* of *O Canada* has winged away on the midnight air, over a quarter of the membership can still stand up and offer to fight any country that says that Plug MacFarland is a liar.

Strong, dark feelings. But the fact is, the great Silver Flyer-Lumberman classic of 1962 was no punk hockey match. Not at all. As anybody over in Mt. Pocock can tell you, it was one of the last great stands of rough-town individualism against the relentlessly rising tide of modern mass-produced conformity and sissy-ness. - Rough-towners, you see, don't like anything conformist, or groupish, or over-organized. They didn't like it then, and they don't like it now. They don't like systems, they don't like being told what to do, and they don't like advanced planning or calculation. It strikes them as sneaky and cheap.

"Just look at them Russians," Plug will say darkly.

"And look at it this way, chief," Plug will add. "Once upon a time in this great north country, a young lad could just lace up the blades, grab some lumber, and straight off over the boards. Then – *whammo*! - all heck might break loose! Jeez! – what the hell, eh? Talk about fun! Boys, a young lad had to get sharp quick. It was all pure talent, just like God intended, none of this sneaky spying around and trying to start up hockey schools and teachin' stuff and training like it was in the Army again!"

"But nowadays ....," Plug shakes his head. "Law and order everywhere. A big game, for instance, they make you play it in some neutral, outa-town barn. They even make you bring in outside Refs, like your own people weren't trustworthy or something. – They expect you to play fair and square with the other team, even though everybody knows the guy's out to scrub you good the second the rubber's dropped! - Now is that logical? Is it? It's just more of this silent surrender, the whole country's getting full of it. Take all them clowns up in Toronto Queens Park. What they all need is a swift kick.

And Plug was right again.

Because, you see, there is nothing rough-towners hate more than the sheep-like conformity of corporate hockey, central governments, Queens Park clowns, and the South Middlesex Silver-Flyers.

The fact is, the Silver Flyers stood for everything rough-towners hate in modern hockey. The Flyers were one of those new, slick, tight-pattern hockey clubs. They were trained to skate forwards and backwards at a whistle, like trained seals. They had *two* coaches behind the bench, a fancy flip-page animation play-book that made blurry sort of motion pictures, and a dressing-room chalk-board painted up to look exactly like an ice-surface, with blue lines and face-off circles and the whole thing.

Worse, those little smart-alecks were smug and self-conceited. You know the types - they all came out of one of those new hoity suburbs that were starting to sprawl out from the great city of London, Ontario, newfangled places where people had to live in American-style ranch-houses with aluminum screen-doors and where there's no upstairs and where the garage is cemented right onto the side of the house, instead of sitting a-ways down the back lane by the chicken coops, where it's supposed to be. Those boys thought they were pretty smart. They had two complete sets of uniform, they were sponsored by a ritzy three-location dough-nut franchise, and they travelled out of town in their own chartered bus, feeding themselves on orange pop and playing four-handed Euchre like little princes.

- But in contrast, in a more decent and normal manner of living, just a few miles west down the Kings Highway 2, and then a certain distance northward, there lay:

MT. POCOCK
Pop. 3500
Home of Highlife Canners Ltd.
LIONS: 2nd Wed. Queens Hotel
INDUSTRY WELCOMED

Anybody who ever travelled Ontario in the old days knows Mt. Pocock. It was one of those fierce and sleepy little towns deep down in the peninsula of Southwestern Ontario, some miles west of the great city of London. Before the 401 Superhighway went through to Windsor, everybody knew that road. And even today, if you travel out the old King's Highway 2, over the farmlands and the creek flats and through the high-fronted towns and villages, and if you know the right side-roads, pretty soon you'll be there.

A few scattered houses and a leafy curve in the highway mark the first outcroppings of the town, and soon you'd bump over the railroad spur by Gough's Lumber Yard and pass the dusty ramp of the Fair/Square Feed Mill – and then you'd be right on Colborne Street, the long main street strung out for a quarter-mile or so, backed by a dozen or more side-streets of compacted clay, which ramble off in various directions to the outlying barley, hay and alfalfa fields.

The town of Mt. Pocock's high-fronted, turn-of-the-last-century commercial centre may seem a bit seedy and un-showy to the passing stranger – but to those in the know, Colborne Street is a financial hive; and any day except Sunday or Wednesday afternoon, farmers and people from as far away as Morpeth Corners, Gormley Centre, North Dunoon Station, or even Bushey-Bagot Hill, will flock to Mt. Pocock to spend currency as though it is going out of style. That is because Mt. Pocock is – and has been for nearly a hundred and forty years – the commercial heart of the township of North Dunoon.

Mt. Pocockians are a proud, serious, and self-reliant people. Anything worth knowing, they teach themselves – and they always like their own way best. They do not take instruction lightly. And although they are slow to rile, they never forget a slight upon their customs and ancient pioneering heritage. It is no wonder, then, that Crunch Routledge's cowardly insinuations stirred up their wrath. In their view, the South Middlesex Silver Flyers were *parvenus* from some rootless suburb, trying to compensate for their lack of culture with slick new methods and guile. Those boys were upstarts.

By contrast, Gough's Lumber and Building Supply, the Mt. Pocock Pride, stuck to the old traditions and to rough-town amateurism, with fierce devotion. They never practiced. They were bored to tears by the Silver Flyers' modern, namby-pamby, tic-tac-toe stuff. In Mt. Pocock, a more heroic style had always prevailed; a boy just went over the boards and bashed away for himself. A true Lumberman never passed unless he got himself into deep personal trouble – and even then, he generally preferred to die at his post before giving up the puck.

And so dazzling glory or abominable shame rode on every play. - Boys, said Plug MacFarland, on a hockey night in Mt. Pocock you might see amazing stick-handling feats, desperado shots unloaded from any place on the ice, at any time, and human battering-rams hurling themselves into every action in the finest rough-town tradition. Talk about individualism!

And skating! – the only imports on the Mt. Pocock side were Wilf Pratt from the nearby hamlet of Morpeth Corners, and the two Van Hoof brothers from up the Third Line. The imports had learned their style on Bungman's Creek, whereas the town talent traditionally came up from the gritty, hummock-studded ice of Gough's Gravel Pit. And so there were two distinct skating styles. The creek veterans were long-striders, who went up the ice in leisurely, sweeping glides and who usually coasted in upon the enemy blue line with both eyes glued to the ice, watching for air-pockets. The true town-bred Mt. Pocockians, on the other hand, could be picked out by any knowledgeable observer by their determined, scrambling, hopscotch stride. Even on indoor ice, true Mt. Pocockians were always unconsciously dodging earth hummocks and stray patches of gravel – and so they did not so much skate as toe-jerk up the ice in an erratic running scramble, three short hops forward, two sudden lurches to one side. But in confined quarters, they were amazing, choppy little stick-handlers, often scoring improbable goals by unexpected, wobbly lunges from a pack of defenders.

And the brains behind the bench? Plug MacFarland, of course, who chewed White Owl cigars and drove the big tow-truck for Farley's Imperial Esso Garage, located at the corner of Maitland and Brock, right across the street from the Queen's Hotel. According to some Mt. Pocockians, Plug MacFarland was the shrewdest hockey mind in six counties. Everything he knew about the game, he had learned from experience and long rough-town tradition. And although it is true that Plug had once been propped up behind the Greys in the old Maple Leaf Gardens, that was during Plug's locally-famous bus-excursion and lost weekend at the Ford Hotel, Toronto. -So naturally, not much of that study of the modern, professional game had rubbed off on him or contaminated his native intuition of the sport. Which was just as well. For Mt. Pocockians have no time for the scientific playbooks, pattern drills and flip-page photo booklets used by modern corporate hockey and the South Middlesex Silver Flyers. That was all gimmickry and just-pretend, said Plug. There's only one way to learn the game – the same way people learn to swim in Mt. Pocock: somebody just flings them into the deeps, down at the swimming-hole in Bungman's Creek.

And so the Lumbermen's only weekly workout was a hair-raising hacking-match against the notorious Mt. Pocock Senior D's – the blackest, paunchiest, and most fearsome senior team in the peninsula. The black Seniors were outstanding teachers. Some were masters of stick-fighting, some of clutch-and-grab and verbal intimidation. Plug himself, of course, had been a rock on the senior defence for over a decade and was master of the lumbering blueline-spear and the corner-elbow. Such were the lessons of the master. And the little Lumbermen were fast studies.

Gough's Lumbermen, Plug said with a fond smile, knew how to take care of themselves. They were ready for the best the Flyers could throw at them.

"Whatever they wanta try,' said Plug, "my lads can go one better.

And so it proved, when Game Time finally arrived.

2.

It was a cold and frosty evening in early spring as the Silver Flyers' chartered bus came stealthily across the farmlands of North Dunoon, en route to the fatal contest.

Mt. Pocock was ominously quiet. The Victorian houses on Colborne Street were darkened, with only a dim kitchen light showing through the back porches. Downtown, the high-fronted stores and commercial buildings were locked up for the night. A meagre yellowish light burned upstairs in the lawyer's office, and a few people sat in the New Canton Cafe – but otherwise the town seemed deserted. No one was on the street; the tow-truck sat dead in the dark forecourt of Farley's Imperial Esso Garage; and the Mt. Pocock Post Office and Masonic Hall was dark.

But the streetlights were turned on early on Maitland Street – for Maitland Street is the road of glory that leads through the back streets past Pocock Park, past the Mt. Pocock water tower and pumping station, to the Lorne Pocock Memorial Arena, where every night in winter immortality is to be won or lost at the drop of a rubber puck.

Of course, the Lorne Pocock Memorial is not a showy place. Set down in the dark creek flats at the back of town, it is a ramshackle rusty Quonset building made of corrugated tin and iron. Dirty snowbanks are heaped around its low walls, and a gravelled parking area, full of tilting hydro poles, sprawls silently before it. The main entrance is a scarred plywood door, badly hinged and lit by a single naked bulb hanging from a goose-neck of tubular steel. The bulb casts a weak, yellowish light into the gloom.

Traditionally, an hour before game time, the Lorne Pocock will be deserted. Nobody is around. There is not an Edsel or a battered Dodge pickup in the parking lot. The only sound is a cold night wind blowing up from the willows in the creek flats. Inside, too, the place is as desolate and silent as world's end. The hidden bowels of the arena are heavy with darkness. The dank smell of sweat and frozen moisture and overheating fills the entry ramp. A great emptiness fills the dome of the rink, where a single dim bulb burns high up in the girders, high over centre ice, casting an eerie glow over the battle flags and the bunting and the faded regimental colours of the North Dunoon volunteers. At the north end, the clock in the scoreboard is stopped dead. And the mystic ice surface itself, lying silently behind its thick mesh fences, gives off a spectral misty light.

Naturally, a visiting team of young fellows who still sleep at home with a night-light may tend to huddle as they edge into that eerie silence. And when they see that the ice-surface is still covered with the snow of the afternoon's Community Skate, they may nervously begin to wonder if there has been a mistake. Their hearts may become uneasy; they may secretly shoot Big Bob Little, the assistant coach and business manager, doubtful looks. Perhaps they have come on the wrong night. Perhaps Big Bob has made a scheduling mistake again. And soon, perhaps, a sort of confusion creeps in, as the team mills around in the chilly shadows, gawking at the enemy rink and whispering among themselves.

- Well, it is an unfortunate fact that Gentleman Jim Archambault, the Flyers' coach, later made the cheap claim that the whole thing was a typical rough-town strategy, designed to stop the old adrenalin-flow dead in its tracks. - But nonsense, says Plug MacFarland, with a pained look on his face, that is all sour grapes and beeswax. Besides, on that late March night in 1962, all Big Bob Little or anybody else had to do was to clear his throat a few times, step right into the darkened rink and call out bravely: *"Hal-looo! Hal-loo, Mt. Pocock!"*

And straight away, fair and square, a glimmer of light appeared at the far end of the rink. A thin door banged. Footsteps echoed through the empty building, until the Flyers could make out a gruff voice, grumbling and complaining as it approached.

And then a wiry old man wearing a long-peaked plaid cap and a frayed blue cardigan stumped straight out of the gloom, frank as can be, and squinted straight at the equipment bags and hockey sticks dumped on his rubber matting.

Clear as the honest light of day and all above-board, it was old Annan Lawrie, the rink manager.

"What'yez want?" growled old A.L. frankly. "Who let all 'yez little buggers in here?"

A nervous guilty laugh ran through the Flyers organization. And when Big Bob Little stiffly pulled out his league papers and explained about the big Final Game that night, old Annan made no sneaky attempt to conceal or mute his skepticism.

"*Hockey* game?" he said, raising one eyebrow. "And you were figurin' t'play in *here*, were ya?"

Old A.L. chuckled mirthlessly.

"And I guess ya got a name for yerselves, have ya?" he asked sardonically. "Or is this here the Dee-troit Red Wings?"

And he stared at the assembled Flyers with amused irony, until they began to shift and feel strangely ashamed of themselves.

"We're South Middlesex," Big Bob explained with some heat.

"What?"

"South Middlesex!"

"*Middle*-sex?"

Old A.L. chuckled to himself for a moment. Then he scratched a sulphur match on the wall and slowly re-lit his cigar butt, studying Big Bob.

"Well, yer too early Middle-sex," he said flatly. "Game don't start for an hour."

And then, grumbling to himself, he shuffled off into the darkness to see if he could find the Flyers a dressing-room.

"Well come on!" he growled over his shoulder. "Don't stand there gawking like school-girls."

It is Tradition in the rough-towns that the visiting team is always given the worst dressing-room in the building. Nobody knows how this custom started, but it is always observed. The Flyers' room was a small dank box, with little heat, no coat-hooks, a cramped L-shape, a broken door and a pair of rickety benches – most of the players had to sit on the concrete floor, tangled in one-another's equipment. Elbows jutted into faces. Shin pads and garters got lost. Tempers flared. And then the traditional Mt. Pocock heckling squad arrived at the open door: a rotation of small, ferret-faced little boys, sniggering and offering the standard demoralizing insults, such as: "*Nyaaah, South Middlesex.*"; "*Hello, Girls!*"; and "*Did ya bring yer mommies with ya?*"

Then it was the local league representative who came in and demanded, provocatively, to check the team list against the birth certificates. The referee stuck his head in to ask if the Flyers had a spare puck which he could borrow. The league representative argued that it seemed to him that the great Brookes was ineligible. The time-keeper came in to arbitrate the dispute. The room filled with various Mt. Pocockians, official and unofficial, all waving their arms and contradicting each other. Somebody said the game should be defaulted. The referee came back and asked if anybody had seen his whistle. The Mt. Pocock Superintendent of Public Works tried to deliver a welcome on behalf of somebody. Big Bob Little had his brief-case open on a bench and was heatedly jabbing his finger at various documents. Coach Archambault, who had a slow fuse, began to pace neurotically and to punch one fist mechanically into the gloved palm of his left hand.

In other words, it was just a standard rough-town opening gambit.

Because, you see, a hockey game is not just a shinny match in the rough towns. It is St. George and the out-of-town Dragon, fought on ice. And if you should ever be foolish enough enter a rough-town arena on a Friday night, in pursuit of the Purina Cup, you must not naively expect to play only the local talent. - No, you must expect to do battle with the entire town, to the bitter death.

See, it's not so much that the rough-town people just like to win. It's that they just don't like to lose.

And meanwhile, the rough-town people were arriving. Headlight beams swept across the arena front, and cars and pickup trucks were filling the gravel parking lot. Inside, too, everything was carnival and light. People were crowding the entrance ramp. People milled around the Lions Club snack-bar, holding steaming coffee cups. Men, women and children were pushing through the crowded foyer and up into the wooden stands which surrounded the ice-surface.

The ice-surface had been freshly flooded, and even at that moment old Annan Lawrie was trundling off the ancient watering-cart. The ice-surface gleamed under the illumination of the rink's hanging lights – and not two minutes later, old A.L. slid out the heavy net frames to scattered applause. At the far end of the rink, somebody clambered up an iron ladder and climbed into the little box behind the scoreboard. The old caged clock was reset. A hand slipped out from a little window and hung two painted boards on the pegs, so that the board read Home: 0 Visitors: 0. - Cheers for the first, half-hearted boos for the second. The stands began to fill seriously now. The time-keeper and official scorer, Druggist Michelson, slid and slithered across centre ice and climbed over the boards into the penalty box, again to good-humoured and knowing applause. But when the night's referee skated out from the end gate, the place began to come alive. - Long jeering boos and razzings – but all in good humour, of course, because the local official for the big Final that night was young Earl Oliphant, Earl Oliphant's boy. Earl Jr. was a local favourite and idol of the girls, once invited to the Toronto Marlborough training camp and considered the athletical prodigy of Mt. Pocock. Earl was a bit of a dandy, with a duck-tail, polished Tacks, and a much-admired green and yellow team-jacket, covered in crests and badges: 'OHA Junior C World Champs, 1958'; 'Pole Vault'; 'Captain, R. Wing'; 'Softball Finalist', and that sort of thing. Needless to say, young Earl put on a little unstudied show of fancy skating, zipping around the ice backwards to check the nets and giving a little insouciant wave to the girls from Henry Pocock District Collegiate.

And then there was a hush in the crowd. Heads craned. A movement of colour was detected at the far end of the rink, in a dim corridor.

And then it began! A stamping of feet on the wooden stands, rising like thunder and growing in volume until it shook the rafters!

The teams were coming onto the ice!

The South Middlesex Silver Flyers came out flying. Round the ice they tore, their gold and white uniforms crisply flashing. What an exhibition of precision and pattern! What style and discipline! Short sharp passes flew back and forth.

-Thunderous boos from the stands and a massive show of yawning.

Gough's Lumber and Building Supply, the Mt. Pocock Pride, of course, straggled out in twos and threes, as the whim took them, and stood around at the end of the rink leaning on the boards and spitting.

Need it be said? Fierce individualism marked the Lumbermen. They wore bits and pieces of uniform, of every colour and description. Wally Unger, the captain, wore one green and one yellow stocking, both darned with thick blue wool. His Mt. Pocock sweater, handed down through his family, was in tatters. Little Gordie Fairweather, the right defenceman, wore his married brother's huge hockey pants – they hung down a foot over his knees and flapped like luffing sails. Baldy Turner (aged 13) was held together by patches of black friction tape. Three of the forwards wore the sort of moth-eaten tuques which had not been seen in an urban hockey game since the Great Depression. Like some tribe of head-hunters, most of them had painted and decorated their hockey sticks with zig-zags and alternating bands of red and black paint, like war-clubs. Six of the fourteen players, including the goal-tender, insisted on wearing the number 9, in adulation of Gordie Howe. Bert Thomas, the gawky left-winger, wore ski-mittens stuffed with cotton wool and he had frugally taped his stick from blade to butt with dirty grey adhesive-tape, to protect the good wood. - But the star of the whole show was Four-Eyes Hardy, the bespectacled and padded-up goaltender. Four-Eyes wore a baseball catcher's chest-protector outside his sweater and a catcher's mask decorated with a turkey feather. He had made his own goaltending stick from a scrap of plywood and a broken shaft. And although he was only 14 years old, he kept a half-smoked Export cigarette butt over one ear, both as a good luck charm and a supposed refreshment between periods – but this was only a swaggering pose which Four-Eyes had copied from the Mt. Pocock black Seniors. Because Four-Eyes would never have actually dared to smoke the thing, or his mother would have tanned his backside. As for his other armament, he had a first-baseman's softball trapper on his catching hand, capable of covering a good square foot of net. His pads were museum pieces, thin ribbed things like cricket pads, of cracked brown cowhide – flakes of which fell off from time to time when he took a hard shot.

-And then a louder roar went up. Plug MacFarland was making his way around the alley to the bench, showered with friendly arm-punches and jovial abuse from the partisan fans. Plug took up his position behind the bench, tilted back his fedora and gave the thumbs-up sign to young Earl Oliphant. The whistle blew. The game began. A massive hooting noise went up from the crowd, boots stomped on the wooden stands, and a battalion of old Legionnaires began to pound the boards at centre ice and to look dangerously out from under their service berets.

Well ... nobody remembers the First Period much. Everybody said it was pretty dull stuff. The Flyers got 3 or 4 lucky goals, but everybody in Mt. Pocock agrees that nothing much else happened.

Disaster struck the Lumbermen at the first face-off. While centre-man Wally Unger sawed at the ice, the great Brookes of the Flyers tipped the puck between his legs and skipped around him into open ice, with only the defence pair to beat.

Baldy Turner promptly fell down, leaving little Fairweather to defend. - Now little Fairweather was obstinate and vain. In spite of explicit injunctions from Plug MacFarland, he would insist at such moments on trying to skate backwards – an art he had never mastered. As the great Brookes broke to the blue line, little Fairweather pumped his arms and legs and wiggled his hips vigorously, trying to get some momentum going – but whipping heavily from side to side, the sheer ponderation of his brother's enormous hockey-pants set up a centrifugal force which spun him around three times before he crashed to the ice. Brookes was in alone on goal! With a fierce leer, the great Brookes drew back his blade for the slap-shot – at which point, Four-Eyes Hardy panicked and abandoned the net.

1-0 for the Flyers! Time: Six Seconds of the First Period.

A loud howl of discontent from the crowd. Abuse for the cowardly Four-Eyes. Popcorn boxes showered on his head. His team-mates gathered around in a hostile mood and proceeded to cuff him on the head. Heated words followed. Four-Eyes blamed his defence-men for incompetence. They charged him with abandoning his post under fire. Four-Eyes offered to fight little Fairweather. -The referee broke it up, threatening penalties. After some jostling, the Lumbermen moved off sullenly, glaring at the unfortunate goaltender and promising retribution, immediately following the game. Four-Eyes skated back to his net with an injured pout and, when no one was watching, made a rude gesture.

Again, they faced off. The Lumbermen were more fortunate this time. Flailing away, Unger accidentally smacked the puck free to Bert Thomas – who quickly unloaded it down the ice at the Flyers' goaltender. Goaltender Tooley scooped it off to his right defence, just as three Mt. Pocock forwards and Baldy Turner came charging into the crease to rough him up. Big Tidham on the Flyers' right defence put a long pass up to Smithers at the centre line – and suddenly the Flyers had a three-on-one, with little Fairweather again the boy in the breach! -But this time little Fairweather had anticipated! He turned tail and skated for his own end as fast as his little legs could carry him. Skating forwards, little Fairweather was pretty good. He beat it back to his own blue line well ahead of the Flyers' attack – but then, foolhardily, in mid-stride he suddenly spun to face his attackers – tried to go into reverse as he crossed the blue line. He went curving off into the corner at terrific speed, completely out of control as though he had been on rails and landed against the corner boards in a crumpled heap of hockey pants.

2-0 Flyers, at the 1:23 mark.

Boos from the crowd. Popcorn boxes showered this time indiscriminately. Four-Eyes Hardy came waddling out of his nets, banging his big goal-stick on the ice to notify his team of his profound sense of betrayal. Was he to stop the entire Flyers team all by himself? Turner was replaced on defence by Norm Tuttle. The referee threatened delay of game and called for the face-off at centre ice. The fans hissed and made noises of displeasure.

At the 12-minute mark, after a long shift, the Flyers dumped the puck into the Mt. Pocock end and went for a line-change. Back on the ice and from behind his own net, little Fairweather sized up the situation swiftly and decided the moment was right to take command. Refusing to pass to anyone, he tried to come out alone, right in front of his own net. There he was met by fresh enemy forecheckers. Nothing daunted, little Fairweather turned and threw a smart back-pass to Four-Eyes in the goal.

3-0 Flyers, as little Fairweather was again howled to the bench.

The rest of the period continued to be a goaltenders' duel. But with only minutes left in the first frame, the Lumbermen came alive and started pressing in the Flyers' end. The puck squirted out of the corner to Shorty Harris, who was parked alone in front of the net.

"*Shoot! Shoot!*" howled the crowd.

In that kind of situation, Shorty liked the slap-shot. So he wound up with a terrific backswing – and fanned on the puck. Alertly, goaltender Tooley charged out of the crease and cleared the loose puck the length of the ice. It went right to Four-Eyes, who was leaning idly on the cross-bar, examining his catching glove.

4-0 for the Flyers.

Howls and execrations. Plug MacFarland called a time-out. Four-Eyes was summoned to the bench and publicly stripped of his equipment, much to his shame.

"Take over, Fairweather," said Plug.

Minutes later, Four-Eyes Hardy was transformed into a plump defenceman, and little Fairweather was in the twines, taking his warm-ups with his usual showy style.

Mercifully, the period ended only a minute or two later, with the Mt. Pocock Pride down 4 goals. -Oh, it is true that Big Bob Little later tried to claim that the First Period ended 2 minutes early, just when the great Brookes had another breakaway. But that cheap shot, says Plug MacFarland, is only poor sportsmanship and sour grapes - everybody knows that rough-town score-clocks keep only approximate time. - That's why the referee brings his own wrist-watch.

"I think we're getting them worried now, boys," Plug said in the dressing-room. "Now get out there this next period and keep the pressure on."

You see, nobody in the rough towns ever worries much about the First Period. Everybody knows that the Lumbermen are just restraining and pacing themselves while they check out the opposition and find out what kind of game the referee wants to call. Besides, being down only 4 goals after a whole period of play is bound to give a rough-town team confidence – so nobody was at all surprised to see the momentum start to change in the next period.

The Flyers did not even open the scoring in the Second Period until the 8-minute mark – and even that was a soft goal.

"Power-play," Plug MacFarland shrugs. "What the darn heck, I got my six best players in the penalty box, eh?"

But there was no doubt that the tide began slowly to turn in the Second Period, and that the rough town style began to emerge.

The second innings (Crunch Routledge complained next day in BEHIND THE TWINES) *was your typical ploughboy clutch-and-grabber … hooks, elbows, the whole shee-bang, mother … worst offender was Hardy, who came up with 14 in the box, including a misconduct for bench-mouth … but even the ol' Cruncher has got to admit that he could see the Mt. Pocock* auto da fe *starting to get results… the Fancy Flyers showed the first signs of unravelling as the hackers set 'em up for the final 20 …*

In the rough towns, you see, nobody worries much about the Second Period. Oh, the fans boo and jeer a little, just to get into the spirit – but everybody knows that the Second Period is a period of disruption. So the Lumbermen took a few penalties? Well, that's just the price of the tactic. Everybody knows it takes a few trips to the box for the Lumbermen to work their magic. But there is no need to worry; the Mt. Pocock *joie de vivre* is infectious – you can see it working right before your eyes. Brookes misses a few passes. Smithers keeps looking nervously over his shoulder. The Flyers' kid-line comes out of the corners covered in horrible black and blue pinch-marks. And big Tidham suddenly slashes Wilf Pratt across the shin pads, on the weak excuse that Pratt had persisted in sly butts in the crease area – it all starts to unravel. The Flyers got only one more goal that period, their sixth.

But the full onslaught is yet to come. Because, you see, in the rough towns the first two frames are merely World Wars I and II. Whereas the Third Period is Armageddon.

The Mt. Pocock apocalypse started the minute the final whistle of the Second Period blew.

As the Flyers stepped off the ice *en route* to their dressing-room, they were blocked by old Annan Lawrie, the rink manager.

"Yer turn to clean the ice, fellas," he informed them with a toothless grin.

Big Bob blinked. "Clean the ice?"

"Well sure," shrugged old A.L. "The other fellas did it after the last period."

"They did?"

"Why sure."

There is no point going into the whole sordid story. In the rough towns, the visitors always clean the ice before the last period. You can argue until you're blue in the face, but the rough towners will just shrug.

"Suit yerselves," old Annan Lawrie will say, "yer the fellas got to play on it."

And you don't have to be a brilliant hockey-mind to understand which team will benefit from an uncleaned surface.

"We're doing this under protest!" said Big Bob. "I want you to know that! I intend to lodge a protest!"

"Well sure," shrugged old Lawrie, wandering off. "Don't blame ya – can't say I'd want to do it myself."

Rough-town ice-cleaning equipment, of course, is not the slick lightweight stuff you see nowadays in the Canadian Tire Store. Rough-town shovelling equipment is home-made and extra heavy, to ensure durability. In Mt. Pocock, they use heavy ploughs bolted and welded up out of cast iron and steel pipe, which take two men to heave.

The fans are always delighted. "Put yer backs into it, girls!" they shout like Captain Bligh.

The one-minute warning whistle blew just as the Silver Flyers got back to their room and slumped exhausted on the benches and floor. Gentleman Jim Archambault was so furious he could not speak.

Then the tempest broke. What happened to the poor South Middlesex Silver Flyers in the Third is shameful to tell. The Mt. Pocock mob was on its feet and howling. A few hundred-more people seemed to have crowded into the stands. The building rocked. Thunderous boos for the Flyers. -And then out came the Lumbermen, recharged and skating like demons! A roar of exultation from the friendly crowd – at last!

"*PO-COCK! PO-COCK! PO-COCK!*" roared the fans.

"Okay, boys,' said Plug MacFarland. "You can open her up now. No quarter. Four-Eyes, get back in the nets. And stay awake this time."

Four-Eyes Hardy skated to the pipes and saluted the crowd.

A thrill went through the home town arena. At last, the battle was truly on!

And it was! From the face-off, Unger hooked the skates out from under Brookes and made off with the puck, running erratically down centre ice, stick-handling like a fiend.

"Wally! Wally!" shouted Bert Thomas, breaking into the clear on the left wing.

But Wally was doing his stuff. The puck was a blur on his blade, his eyes were glued to the ice. Macdonald was waiting for him at the blue line, with a shattering hip-check.

A horrible howl went up from the crowd. Cowardly assault! Blood and vengeance were demanded. - And so, Earl Oliphant Jr. had no real choice in the matter. He bowed to massive Popular Demand and sent Macdonald to the box for two minutes.

"*EARL! EARL! EARL!*" chanted the fans appreciatively.

Gentleman Jim scrambled up onto the Flyers' bench, hollering apoplectically – but of course nobody paid any attention. People in Mt. Pocock were beginning to get a little tired of that guy's constant carping and complaining. Away went Macdonald to the cooler.

It was then that Plug MacFarland made an important psychological move. He called Four-Eyes Hardy out of the nets and to the bench – and put out an extra attacker. This unorthodox move seemed to rattle the Flyers. They looked up at the time clock in confusion, then at the empty net at the other end of the rink. And the Lumbermen were not long in capitalizing – from the face-off in the South Middlesex end, Wally Unger banged the puck behind the net. Big Tidham went in to check him. It was then that Wally gave a masterful demonstration of the Mt. Pocock gravel pit close-quarters technique. He clubbed the puck into Tidham's skates. Tidham scrambled to find it. Wally banged the puck into the goal frame. Tidham had to change directions. Wally banged it into his skates again. In confusion, big Tidham tried to turn two ways at once and got himself tangled up. Again off the goal frame. The last swivel was too much for Tidham. His feet tangled, down he went, as Wally chopped the puck through his legs and came out from behind the net, elbows and knees pumping furiously and the rubber dancing back and forth. In panic, big Tidham hooked out his stick and tripped him. Wally Unger took three stumbling steps before he went down – and then, just as he was toppling, he threw his arms around the Flyers' goaltender. The pair sprawled in the crease, Wally effectively pinning the goalie. The puck bounced loose in front.

At that point, Regulus Van Hoof, who could raise the puck, walked in and lifted it into the net.

The place went wild! The Mt. Pocock crowd was on its feet roaring and stamping in triumph. Regulus Van Hoof was lifted up and carried twice around the rink, while the grateful crowd showered him with applause.

"NUMBER NINE! NUMBER NINE! NUMBER NINE!" shouted the fans.

Well! The floodgates had opened! - Naturally, the Flyers made a protest about the player in the goal crease. But Earl Jr. was no fool. Unger hadn't tripped himself. So he sent big Tidham off to join MacDonald in the penalty box.

6-1! - And the Lumbermen had that all-important first goal!

Well, any smart hockey fan could see that the Lumbermen had the momentum going for them now. And Gentleman Jim, who knew about the rough towns, began to look a little desperate. - And no wonder! At about the 4-minute mark, Turner made a smart pass straight up-ice to Bub Wilcox, who was straddling the centre line. Breakaway! And there is nobody in all North Dunoon more deadly on the one-on-one than Bub Wilcox. He had Tooley going four directions at once like a yo-yo – "just like he had that puck on a string," says Plug. *Bango!* 6-2 Flyers.

Can you believe it? Archambault was instantly claiming that the Lumbermen had too many men on the ice – that Bub Wilcox had jumped over the boards from the bench to take the pass. – But, of course, when it came to getting serious, he couldn't prove a thing – there wasn't a single witness to back him up in the whole Mt. Pocock arena.

That's the way it starts in the rough towns. Less than 7 minutes later, the Mt. Pocock Pride had bagged another 3. Amazing! The Lumbermen barged around the ice like boys possessed, hacking and chopping at anything that moved. They cut down rushes at centre. They crowded the blue line and hurled themselves in front of shots. They rocketed into corners with their sticks and elbows high – and the Flyers fell apart.

"LAY THE LUMBER ON THAT NUMBER 6, WALT!"
"WRACK 'EM UP, BOYS!"

Bang! A deflection goes in off Norm Tuttle's skates as he clutches Tooley's stick. Crash! A pileup in front of the Flyers' net, and in the confusion Murray Van Hoof manages to glove the puck to Hughie Greene, who gloves it under Tooley. Bang, Flash! Georgie White collides with Brookes, the puck is coughed up and Ronny Parson gobbles it up at centre and slap-shoots it at the goal. The shot goes wide, but takes a funny bounce off the back boards, caroms out at a freak angle and catches Tooley going the wrong way, leaving the net wide open! Four-Eyes Hardy, who has left his defensive position in order to score goals, makes a desperate dive and chops the loose puck at the Flyers' goal! He misses! Shorty Harris has another swipe and fans on the disk! Four-Eyes gets another whack! It goes into big Tidham's skates, and Tidham accidentally kicks it into his own net!

Mayhem! Mt. Pocock goes wild!

"*FOUR-EYES! FOUR-EYES! FOUR-EYES!*" they scream in wild adulation, all past sins forgiven.

6-5 Flyers! With over six minutes to go! Plenty of time! The Lorne Pocock Memorial Arena is rocking on its foundations! People are jumping up in the aisles and people are climbing the meshes behind the nets! A battalion of the Mt. Pocock Legion has pulled off their coats in wild excitement and are ready to fight any other armed force in the place! Plug MacFarland is yelling behind the bench, while the fans lean dangerously out of the stands to thump him on the back in congratulations! The Lumbermen are all on the ice, mobbing and punching Four-Eyes!

5 goals in fourteen minutes! Was there ever anything to beat it in the history of all North Dunoon? The South Middlesex team is shell-shocked. They stand around their bench dazed. Everything has suddenly fallen apart. The uproar goes on for a solid five minutes, and it is another five before old Annan Lawrie can find enough volunteers to bring out the big ploughs and clear the ice of debris.

"*Stay cool! Stay cool!*" Gentleman Jim pleads, grabbing the great Brookes by the shoulder-pads and shaking him until his head threatens to snap off. "*We can't let ourselves get rattled!*" he shrieks, his eyes wild and his lip lathered with foam. "*Can't you see that's what they want?*"

Good advice – but is it too late? It is always rough-town strategy to whip up the pace and the panic.

"Lissen! Lissen!" Gentleman Jim hollers, bringing his boys into a tight huddle. "Now this delay can help us! – Everybody cool out, get your minds together!"

That delay almost cost the Lumbermen the game. The South Middlesex Silver Flyers were a disciplined team. When the whistle blew after a long cooling-out period, the Flyers had regrouped and began to slow down the play. Big Tidham retreated behind his own net with the puck and waited for his team to set up. When Wally Unger, Bert Thomas and Hughie Greene all rushed in to check him, Tidham coolly passed off to Macdonald. And when Unger, Thomas and Greene rushed off in a pack in pursuit of Macdonald, he (equally cool) fed the puck back to Tidham behind the net. An uneasy murmur went through the crowd. Back charged Unger, Thomas and Greene – fanning out this time to box in big Tidham. But suddenly, Macdonald began to move up. In a flash, he had the breaking pass from Tidham, and the Flyers broke out four-strong!

"Get back! Get back!" screamed the crowd to the three trapped forwards.

Too late! The Flyers came blistering across centre, four-on-two. Baldy Turner decided to stand up like a man at the blueline for the classic poke-check – in a flash, the Flyers burned past him – leaving Fairweather again the boy on the burning deck!

"Oh, *no!*" screamed the fans.

They knew whereof they spoke! A decoy pass went to the Flyers' left winger – and taking the bait like a chump, little Fairweather made a twenty-foot charge at the winger on the boards. Boom! Fairweather over the boards and down in a heap, as the pass comes back to centre! Three Flyers in alone in front of the net! Smithers fired a high, hard one to the top corner of the net! Four-Eyes Hardy held his ground as if frozen! - Then, to everyone's astonishment, a loud *crack*! And then the puck hit the end boards with a louder thud and dropped harmlessly behind the net.

And then the brilliant part – at the sound of the puck hitting the boards, Four-Eyes Hardy made an incredibly flamboyant leap into the air, elbow and goal-stick thrown high, and came back down with a triumphant flourish. The puck lay dead behind the net. And returning in the nick of time, Turner golfed it down the ice for a whistle.

Now the Mt. Pocock Lumbermen may not have been outstanding when it came to pattern play, but they knew how to use their heads. The moment the puck was safely cleared, they gathered around Four-Eyes, whacking him across the pads in loud congratulation. The crowd went wild at Four-Eyes Hardy's amazing save, especially those standing right behind his net. People pounded enthusiastically on the wire mesh. The stomping of feet in the stands sounded like thunder.

Coach Archambault was already up on the bench, waving his arms and demanding an inspection of the net. The crowd hooted scornfully. Smithers skated behind the net and poked around in the twines with his stick – and suddenly, he began to protest to the referee. Apparently, as some outside people later tried to claim, he found a large hole in the top corner of the netting.

It was no good appealing to the referee. Earl Jr. just shrugged and said it was the goal judge's decision. Everybody approached the Reverend Dimple, who was sitting on a stool behind the mesh.

"Whaddaya say, Reverend?" asked young Oliphant, slackly chewing his gum.

The Reverend Dimple blinked, startled by this sudden interest.

"In or not?' demanded the referee. "Whaddya think, huh?"

"Well ...," procrastinated that honest gentleman, making an apologetic gesture. In fact, like most of the crowd, he had been so interested in Fairweather's hair-raising rocket trip over the boards, that he had missed the shot.

"Well ... I didn't actually *see* it go in ... but ..."

"No goal!" proclaimed young Earl. He skated to the circle to his left and blew the whistle.

Now a lot of smart people figure it was the heads-up play of Four-Eyes Hardy that saved the game. His classic feint is still remarked on with admiration as a positive inspiration. For one thing, it saved an important goal. For another, Coach Archambault of the Flyers was so enraged by the dismissal of the goal that all the veins stood out in his forehead. He lost control and charged right out onto the ice to challenge the referee. - A few minutes later, he was firmly escorted to the exit by Police Chief Ray Pocock.

"Now I got to admit," says Plug MacFarland, "that we got an extra break there. - I woulda been happy just to steal the goal, eh?"

Now a disciplined pattern-team without a coach to guide it is a crippled team. When play resumed, the Flyers seemed disoriented. Nonetheless, with less than three minutes remaining, the puck bounced loose to the Flyers. Tidham ragged it until his men regrouped. Then he quickly passed up to Poole, who broke fast at centre, made a nifty move at the blue line and wound up for the shot. -Suddenly there was a loud whistle. Everybody stopped play and looked at the referee – and it was then that Bub Wilcox grabbed the abandoned puck and made a solo dash for the Flyers' undefended goal. The Flyers watched him curiously. Tooley yelled and looked confused. Bub was in all alone. Tooley came out in puzzlement and made a half-hearted attempt to block him, but in a flash Bub was around and poking it into the corner. - And the goal-light flashed red!

Pandemonium and confusion! The Lumbermen had tied it up! The comeback of the century, said a banner headline in the Mt. Pocock Plain Dealer next week! Up in the stands, a dozen whistles blew in loud acclamation.

Now in sole charge behind the Flyers' bench, Big Bob was beside himself.

"What's going on?" he demanded, looking frantic and wiping his forehead. "Was that a goal?"

Young Earl just shrugged. Frankly, he too was getting a little ticked-off at the antics from the Flyers' bench.

"Of *course,* it was a goal," he sighed. "You got eyes?"

"But the whistle blew!" Big Bob howled. "The play had stopped."

"Wasn't *my* whistle," shrugged young Earl with massive contempt.

"But .... but ... but ...," Big Bob stuttered.

"See," says Plug MacFarland, "your average robot-hockey-player is just like a trained seal. He hears somebody blow a whistle, his little brain stops working, and he just stops and leaves the puck lay. Somebody up in the stands gives a harmless toot, and these boys pack up and go home."

Well ... no amount of protesting or threatening made any difference. Earl Jr. was adamant. Could *he* be responsible for the whole Mt. Pocock Legion? He was just the referee. What did Big Bob expect the referee to do? - Search everybody in the stands to make sure they hadn't brought any whistles into the game? Be reasonable. If the Flyers had suddenly let down and stopped, was that *his* fault? *He* hadn't told them to do it. Maybe the Flyers should pay more attention to the game at hand and not be gawking around and listening to what the fans were doing in the stands. And furthermore ...

Just then the siren blew to end regulation time. In the excitement somebody had forgotten to stop the clock.

"We got Sudden Death here!" young Earl proclaimed.

Well, it was a shameful ending to a good match-up. Who would have thought the Flyers would turn out to be such sore losers? Young Earl could hardly get them off the ice. The whole team mobbed around him, shouting abuse and threats — and it was a credit to the fair play of young Earl that he decided to ignore the whole thing and hand out no penalties. No, young Earl told the Assembled Press after the game, in his way of figuring it, the best policy was to start off the overtime period even-steven. No disadvantages on either side. Let the two teams settle the matter fair and square – first goal to win the whole shooting-match. Now who could argue with that? The Flyers had the same chance as the Lumbermen – all they had to do was pop the first goal and – hell, the Purina Trophy was theirs. They would have won it fair and square and could go home holding up their heads like champions. As far as Mt. Pocock was concerned, they were ready to forget what had gone before and to look upon the overtime as a whole new fresh start – let bygones be bygones and no hard feelings, eh? What could be more fair?

"Okay, men," said Plug MacFarland in the dressing room, "let's put a cork in this one before 9:30, okay? - I gotta see a man about a horse."

Well, there are some people who claim the South Middlesex Silver Flyers never really had a chance. When they returned to the ice after a short interval, they were a beaten and demoralized team. They had seen a six-goal lead vanish, they had lost their coach, they felt they had been robbed of at least three goals, and Big Bob Little had just delivered a pep-talk that left them all miserable, depressed and feeling futile.

But that's all nonsense, says Plug MacFarland. The game of hockey is like the game of life. Anybody can win. And while you still got the legs, you can still score the goals. And it only takes one good shot to put her away. See, says Plug, there's a lot of people in this country like to lay down and die when things go a little bad. Unlike your true Mt. Pocockians, they got no inner resources to draw upon. Because, see, the game of hockey isn't just a game of shinny. It's a game of character. And a boy who can take the worst the other fella can dish out and still come back with a few tricks of his own – well now, that's a boy worth voting for when he grows up. - And that's what your real rough-town hockey night is really all about, eh?

3.

Well, it was a cold and frosty night in Mt. Pocock when the whistle blew to start the first ten minutes of overtime. A faint moon peeked out of the scattered clouds, casting light on the fields and the willow flats. The town itself was silent. A few lights glimmered in the backstreets, as the moon drifted over the town.

But out at the end of Maitland Street, that ribbon of glory that leads past Pocock Park and the pumping station, the Lorne Pocock Arena was light and bedlam. A low rumble seeped out to the darkened parking lot – but open up that thin plywood door and step into the entry ramp – and what a din and furor met the ears! High up in the rafters, the regimental colours of the North Dunoon volunteers glittered and stirred in the rows of hanging lights, the banks of wooden stands were filled to overflowing with chanting, stamping, pounding, shouting, desperate fans, their breaths steaming into the frosty air. The Purina Cup had been brought out to the penalty box. The old scoreboard at the north end of the rink showed the fatal situation. Home: 6 Visitors: 6 Overtime.

Sudden Death! Can anything sir the hearts of the rough towns more than that apocalyptic phrase? One throw of the dice! One fatal error, one moment of brilliance! This is the real drama that hides behind the sleepy exterior of the rough towns of the world. Sudden Death! Glory or Shame! - And no tomorrow!

Out on the mystic ice-surface, the teams are lined up for the fatal face-off; the crisp gold and white uniforms of the South Middlesex Silver Flyers glitter regally, precise, ordered, disciplined. On the other side, the multi-coloured war array of the Mt. Pocock Pride gleams colourfully. Such pageantry! There is an air of high ritual as Wally Unger coasts into the circle to face off against the great Brookes. The referee's arm is in the air -the whistle blows! - and the puck drops!

Brookes grabs the draw! The puck goes back to Tidham! Tidham passes off to MacDonald – and straight up the ice it goes! Smithers takes a pass and breaks across the Mt. Pocock blueline on the wing!

"*DE-FENCE! DEE-FENCE! DEE-FENCE!*" urges the mighty fevered crowd.

But there is no need to fear. Little Fairweather is at his post – and with a mighty lunge, he hurls himself across the ice and cuts down Smithers at the top of the circle – taking the legs right out from under him! The puck springs free and is gobbled up by Brookes the centre-man, who wheels and looks for Poole cutting to the net. Three sticks flash out with eye-blinding speed – and Brookes is hacked apart before he can make a play! Poole is ridden off into the corner by Baldy Turner, who has a firm clutch on his suspenders.

Now the Lumbermen break out! Wilcox head-mans it to Unger! But Unger is banged off the puck at centre! The Flyers counter-attack as Macdonald returns it up ice to Poole! But -whack! Poole is neatly disarmed, his stick flies across the ice. Fairweather tests a sixty-footer at the Flyers' net – and that is the signal for line changes all around! Fresh troops come pouring over the boards! Short, sharp shifts! Check, check, check! Keep the fresh legs coming! - Back and forth it rages!

'*PO-COCK! PO-COCK! PO-COCK!*" bellows the beast.

And then, at last, it comes: The Moment of Truth.

The puck is shot into the Flyers' end, and the Lumbermen scurry off for a line change! The crowd tenses! The Flyers have a dangerous breathing-space to regroup in their own end! The great Brookes turns and comes sweeping back to pick it up! Round the curve of the corner he mightily sweeps, picking up speed – he will carry it himself! The Lumbermen scramble to plug up the centre, but Brookes feints and sweeps to the left side! Electricity fills the Lorne Pocock Memorial Arena and Community Centre! *This is it!* Everybody senses that the moment is at hand! There is just something in the way that Brookes comes out of his own zone! You can see it in his stride! You can see it in his face! - *He is going to score! Oh no!*

"*CHECK HIM! CHECK HIM!*" scream the fans.

Well ... never count your chickens before they're hatched, says Plug MacFarland. There is always more to a good play than meets the eye ... For just as Brookes is about to reach centre, he makes an error that is always fatal in the rough towns; he sweeps in too close to the boards. The Mt. Pocock Legion Battalion is waiting – and then it comes, in a split second, so fast and so deceptive that you might think your eyes had deceived you. Brookes give a sudden lurch, as if jerked back on a string. The puck squirts loose! Turner jumps up, smartly grabs it and head-mans it to Bub Wilcox who is straddling the enemy blue line! The South Middlesex defence, who had been coming up hard behind Brookes, put on the brakes and try to turn back! Too late! Bub Wilcox is behind them all! *Bub Wilcox is in the clear!*

"*BUB! BUB! BUB!*"

Well ... can there be any doubt about it? There is nobody in all North Dunoon who can do the old razzle-dazzle, the old dipsy-doodle, or the old rinky-dinky-doo better than Bub Wilcox. On a Saturday morning down in Gough's Gravel Pit, Bub Wilcox can take his little sawed-off stick and go through a crowd of 43 opposing shinny players in a snowstorm and still score standing up. There is nobody in the whole peninsula of Southwestern Ontario who can touch Bub Wilcox when it comes to the breakaway.

It was pathetic to watch. Bub just toyed with Tooley, like a cat with a mouse, jerking him to the left, feinting him to the right – had that Flyer goalie dancing on a string, until poor Tooley was nearly crying tears of frustration. And then, just as the Flyer defenders were nearly back upon him, Bub made a very nifty spin-a-rama, just to show the hometown crowd who was in command – and casually backhanded the winner into the low left corner.

Victory!

... Well, you never saw such a let-down team as the Flyers. They just stopped skating and fell down on the ice and bent their heads in shame.

Such a bedlam! People later said that you could hear the horrible exultant howl all the way out to Hardwick's Dairy at Burgsville. People were storming up and down the wooden stands, cheering and screaming. People were crowding down to the boards, banging their fists and kicking their boots on the woodwork. Such a storm of hats and buckle-galoshes you never saw in your life! And why not! The Lumbermen had vindicated the glory and the honour of Mt. Pocock and all the rough towns everywhere!

... Well, that's the true facts and opinions of the night that Gough's Lumber and Building Supply copped the Purina Cup over in North Dunoon in '62. Oh, there were lots of protests about the whole thing, of course. There always are, over in North Dunoon, everybody expects it. But everybody also knows that possession is nine-tenths of the law; and when the South Middlesex Silver Flyers' bus left town an hour later, slinking over the flat farmlands in the darkness, the Cup was already safely locked up and secured in the vault of the Town Clerk's office. And there was no way anybody as going to get it out of there short of armed violence.

A lot of people were disappointed at how the Silver Flyers turned out to be such soreheads. They wouldn't shake hands after the game and they didn't show up for the free cocoa at the little post-game reception given by the Ladies Auxillary over at the United Church basement. They just left town as fast and as rudely as possible.

The Lumbermen didn't care. They just went ahead and drank all the cocoa and ate all the jelly doughnuts themselves. A month later, there was a big Lions Club dinner in honour of the boys. Four-Eyes Hardy was voted Most Valuable Player of the game, just to show there were no bad feelings. Vic's Gentleman's Apparel on Colborne Street put up a free 4-dollar gift certificate for Bub Wilcox, who was the

First Star and High Scorer. Earl Oliphant Jr. was given a fine hand all round and a voucher for a free Lube and Oil Change down at Farleys Imperial Esso Garage. And the Mt. Pocock Legion dipped into its war chest and bought each of the Lumbermen a brand-new green and yellow team jacket, with a big Mt. Pocock town crest on the front. - You could still see Plug MacFarland wearing his a couple of decades later, when he went out on call with the big tow truck from Farleys.

But probably the finest thing to commemorate and honour the Lumbermen was the way the town mayor stood up at the head table and gave a fine long speech saying how the boys had brought new glory to Mt. Pocock and how he personally intended to vote 55 dollars cash money to see that something was done so that the deed would never be forgotten.

And the mayor was as good as his word. The great Flyer-Lumberman contest happened a long, long time ago; but even today, if you go west on the Kings Highway 2, out west of the great city of London, and if you know the side roads, pretty soon you will come to a shady tunnel of maple trees which marks the entrance to the fine old town of Mt. Pocock. And there on the highway, just where the road curves into the trees, there is a big tilting sign which tells the whole story of glory in fading green and yellow paint:

MT. POCOCK
Pop. 3600
HOME OF GOUGH'S LUMBER AND BUILDING SUPPLY
PURINA CUP WORLD'S CHAMPIONS, 1962
LIONS: 2nd Wed Queens Hotel
INDUSTRY WELCOMED

A pretty classy gesture, eh? And why not? That's the way things get done, over in the rough towns.

****

THE 1901 BARNEYVILLE CUP

In all Puddle Township, it was Fergus O'Donnell had the great name of the hockey player - starring at the centre ice position and leading the Barneyville Shamrocks to many a grand victory and to many the fine, glorious sporting trophy.

But for all that, the Barneyville boys had never yet won the Lord Stanley's new silver cup. And the terrible shame and failure of it all had lately begun to oppress Fergus's mind.

"Boys," said Fergus, early the one New Year's morning of 1901, down at the Barneyville pond, "it's many the glorious sporting exploit we've achieved together - and many the grand victory we've seized upon the frozen pond. - But for all that, there's still the one outstanding shinny prize we've failed to capture, entirely, entirely."

At this unexpected news, all the boys stared up in surprise from the snow bank in which they were seated, unbuckling the straps of their rusty skates.

"And what outstanding shinny prize might that be then, Fergus O'Donnell?" enquired Tommy Hankin. "For none of us boys here are aware of any glorious awards still goin', that the noble Shamrocks *haven't* won! - And isn't that so, boys?"

"*Entirely true, Tommy Hankin!*" agreed a proud chorus. "Champions of Puddle! 1896-1900."

"Puddle!" was all that Fergus replied, disparagingly. "Small potatoes, boys."

And he leaned glumly upon his famed, hand-carved, one-piece shinny stick, Ash the Annihilator; and with one thick cowhide mitten he made a gesture of some disdain.

The boys were entirely shocked.

"Now hold the horses right there, Fergus O"Donnell!" protested Owen Smithers. "You're speaking as if the boys had achieved no other recent doughty deeds at all, at all!"

For hadn't the mighty Shamrocks whipped all local competition now, five seasons straight? And weren't they even now, this very morning of the New Year's Day of 1901, again current defending Young Men's Champions of both North Puddle and South Dingle Townships, and of all the frozen lakes and rivers between?

Small potatoes, was it?

"Yes, keep a civil tongue there, Fergus," agreed Rory Burn, who played at the cover-point position. "For was it not only the last week, now, that we triumphed over the fearsome Stumptville Beavers? And all that with being down 5-2, goin' into the second half?"

"True again!" added Bartel Clancy. "And didn't we entirely annihilate the mighty Dumptytown Wanderers, 7-0, only the last month of it? - And that despite travellin' all night in Larry Rooney's heavy logging sled, just to get to the match?"

"Indeed, what more glory do ye *want*, man?" complained Alex Morrison.

"Morrison is right!" the other players agreed loudly. "*Hurrah the Barneyville Boys!*"

For each of the boys was privately thinking it was some nerve of Fergus O'Donnell, to be giving such a low opinion of a grand, fine hockey squad like the Shamrock Seven, true-blue champions, and glorious, manly young athletes who had heaped such eternal glory upon the entire hamlet - and all that, too, while playing the noble shinny game only in their spare times, being young working men with serious jobs to go to of a winter's morning, down at the sawmill, or on their fathers' rocky farms.

For the Shamrocks were a proud team - true young sportsmen and grand amateur athletes, every man (and idols of the local girls.)

But again, Fergus was not impressed.

"Faded memories," he shrugged. "*Local* fame."

"*Local,* d'ye call it?" again protested some of the boys, heatedly. "Local only, is it? And when it's a good thirteen miles and more to Dumpytown through the snow? And nearly the same again to Stumptville – although that's in a different direction entirely?"

Fergus just smiled again, in a rather dismissive manner.

"*Ah, then!*" suggested Emmet Leary sardonically. "But perhaps it's not the noble winter *shinny* the boy's yearning to win at now. But perhaps he's got romantic ambitions for some other lesser, summery, *girly* game. - For might it be, that it's the legendary Prince Albert Memorial for Young Ladies and Gentlemen's Mixed Softball, that he'd be now setting his cap at? And small wonder of it – for didn't we all see the big lad spooning like a bashful idjiot only last Empire Day Picnic, while teaching Mary O'Brien Farrell how to swing the ladies' baseball bat?"

Fergus blushed a fiery red.

"Of *course,* it's never the *Albert,* ye great idiot. – Besides, didn't we nearly win that one too, in the year of Her Majesty Queen Vctoria,'97 - if it hadn't been for Tommy Hankin striking out three times in the 9th, to ruin the rally? - And all that after Maggie-Margaret O'Donovan loading the bases!"

"Well *then,* what the devil *are* you talkin' about?" demanded a chorus. "What's left to win in the wintry shinny, boyo? If it's not local?"

"*Ah!*" Fergus hinted shrewdly, laying a finger aside the nose.

Owen Smithers looked in astonishment.

"*What?* Not local then? "

Fergus merely smiled.

"What, not just the Two Townships Championship? - But then ... surely you're not dreamin' of the All-County Porcupine Platter? - For Barneyville? Never been done, lad!"

"Ah, but then," hinted Fergus slyly, "reflect upon yourselves, young hearties. Is there not something even grander than the sacred Porcupine? Now could that be?"

"Grander than the Porcupine? ... Why that would be ... *No!* Not the East Central Young Gentlemen's Finals? You're dreamin' on a scale like that?"

"Still shootin' her wide of the post, boys," said Fergus ironically, dropping into the true Ontario vernacular. - And then for even greater effect: "Think of the grandest, top sporting prize ever to be had, in all our entire noble Dominion, from Sea to Sea. – And what might that be?"

At this hint, Michael Davies experienced a staggering imaginative shock.

"Hold on there a moment! Don't tell me you're dreaming of ... no, *not the entire Dominion Trophy?*"

Fergus just smiled.

"The *what?*" asked the boys, hardly able to comprehend the gigantic scope of this ambition.

Fergus smiled again.

"*Save the day!*" uttered Davies, "The boy's entirely *mad!* Not the Lord Stanley's new silver cup up in Ottawa! – But you can't be thinkin' about that one, Fergus? - Have you been off with the fairies, boyo?"

"And why would I not?" asked Fergus impatiently. "And isn't it just there for the taking?"

"But that's a famous *challenge* cup."

"The *what* trophy?" inquired several of the boys. "What the devil are you two referring to now?"

"Yes, Question to the House," put in Tommy Hankin. "This Lord Stanley's silver *thingee*, it's some kind of big prize for the shinny-playing, is it now?"

"Not just a prize," said Michael Davies, taking off his spectacles. "But the famous silver punch bowl awarded for the grandest hockey team in all the glorious Dominion, sea to shining sea!"

"No!" objected another shocked chorus of the boys. "Top team in all the land? - Not just Puddle?"

There was a lengthy pause and then a troubled murmur ran about the team.

"- And who exactly might this Lord Stanley fellow be, anyways, when he's at home?" asked Tommy Hankin, who played the Rover and who was always sticking his nose into somebody else's play.

"You great idiot! He's only the top Governor-General of the entire Dominion, up in Ottawa."

"The top Governor-General up in Ottawa, is it?"

"The same."

"No!"

Finally, after chewing his lip and toying with the leather straps of his blades for a long, long moment, Rory Burn looked up and asked the question that was now on the minds of all the boys:

"And it's really this silver championship cup up in Ottawa, the nation's capital, that you're dreamin' of winning, Fergus?"

"Certainly!"

"The silver cup the Governor-General himself is offerin' to the finest hockey team in all the northern land? Would it be that one, then?"

"Of course! The great cup, himself."

"And you're also thinking the Barneyville Shamrocks might be trying to win it then - is that your thought?"

"Yes, man! Why not?"

Now there was even deeper pondering.

Finally, Rory Burn spoke up again.

"But that's an invitational challenge cup, Fergus."

"And so?"

"Well ... we haven't been invited, Fergus. There's the trouble of it."

"-Yes! I mean, a fellow can't just go up to the Governor-General and say he wants to have the great shiny thing, can he? You have to be accepted to play the competition for it, I believe."

"Any senior league champion team can challenge," persisted Fergus, "Any time in a season. It's in the rules."

"Ah, but you might as well challenge the wind, boy."

"Yes, Rory's right there, Fergus," said Michael Davies, standing up and hitching his braces over his woollen shirt. "And besides, even if you did challenge, it's only famous, big-city players that would get the invitation. And who's ever heard of Barneyville and Puddle Township?"

"Boys!" urged Fergus. "It's the whole new era! - This isn't the 19th century anymore!"

"Well, until Midnight last night, it was," observed Tommy Hankin.

"You're just dreamin', Fergus boy."

After that, all the boys had a good laugh at the way Fergus was pulling their legs, with his yarn about the Lord Stanley's Cup.

And soon after, the manly young Shamrocks adjourned their practice for that first New Year's morning of the new century, picking up their skates by their leather straps and shouldering their one-piece, hand-carved sticks and heading off on their separate ways.

But a dejected Fergus remained alone by the ice a good while longer, brooding over the snowy surface of the famed Barneyville municipal shinny pond – and staring away across the nearby marshes and over the icy waters of Big Puddle Lake, to the smoky, wood-fuelled hamlet of Barneyville itself, huddled along the forest shore.

The sleepy hamlet of Barneyville was quiet that mild winter morning of the early new year. But down by the town wharf, tied up and unloading cargo, was the old *DisHon. John A. Macdonald*, the Whig-owned steamer from down the chain of lakes - for it was the brief January thaw, and winter passage on the Big Puddle had re-opened for a week.

Our young hero now sighed sadly, in deep dejection of his vital spirits.

- Alas, this raw, soulless, woodsy, new country. - For without a daring shinny dream to fuel a young lad's natural yearnings for doughtiness and manly deeds, what was in it? Just granite rocks and empty sky, with perhaps a few hundred thousand freshwater lakes and some barky trees thrown in besides. - But aside from all that furniture, what was in it all, if not for the Shinny?

A while longer Fergus remained, brooding by the bush-fringed municipal pond, feeling an emptiness and a sad, ghostly yearning for slapping pucks and cutting blades.

But at last, in resignation - and in a very gloomy mood it was – our lad hoisted his hockey traps and began to trudge himself off homewards, along the marsh edge, hacking his way moodily at frozen bulrushes and cat-tails with his old hockey stick – and occasionally slap-shooting a small clod of frozen grass and earth into the marsh – and not just for the healthy skill-building of it all, as you might imagine, but to vent his general disappointment with the boys.

But as Fergus left the low marsh and began to trudge up a snow-covered bush road, towards the hill that led to his own dad's farm, he spotted Tommy Underhill's big freight waggon, already up ahead, climbing the slippery slope – just come up from the steamer wharf and drawing a heavy load of supplies and mail for the outlying bush settlements.

Tommy's pair of old grey horses were straining mightily to hold to the icy slope -for hard dangerous pulling, it appeared. And sure enough, the over-loaded freight waggon suddenly side-slipped, one wheel catching an icy rut, threatening to tip and topple. But just in time, at a sharp crack of old Tommy's whip, the team pulled more mightily, and the waggon corrected, finally jostling and swaying over the crest of the hill, and soon disappearing down the other side.

Fergus paused for breath, before himself trudging onward.

But when at the very top of the hill, what should Fergus find, but a broken packing-crate and its shattered contents, tumbled out over the roadway - having spilled off the tailboard of the waggon.

"*Tommy boy*!"

But it was too late. Old Tommy was now far away down the other side of the hill and out of hearing.

But then our Fergus spotted something entirely strange. For there, sprawled out on the roadway amid the spillage, was a wee small tiny little fellow - the smallest little fellow Fergus had ever seen!

"*Be-jaysus*!" Fergus exclaimed in surprise. "And who the *divil* are you?" - For the wee feller certainly wasn't local.

Startled, the little man looked up in alarm and tried to scuttle off.

"Niver minding your own business," cried the wee little man, scuttling safely out of reach. "For you'll be getting nothing from me!"

Fergus stared again.

"You were stowed away inside that packing crate?"

"And who's to say I was?" challenged the little fellow. "And where's your witnesses?"

Fergus bent closer, to examine a label pasted onto the broken shipping box.

"Why, it indicates right here, that this particular packing-crate has travelled all the way from over the seas, from the old green country!" he exclaimed in surprise. - "And - *why then!* - so too must have you!"

"*Did I?*" parried the little man evasively. "Maybe I did and maybe I didn't. And who wants to know?"

Fergus stared. Then with a shock, a wondrous realization came upon him. A tiny little fellow from the auld sod, the old green land back home!

"Why, you're one of the *Good Folk*!"

And without a moment's hesitation, Fergus made a dart and an athletic grab for the little fellow. But the little man was too quick and dodged away.

But our Fergus was not champion stick-handler of all North Puddle Township for nothing. Instantly, he whipped out his stick and blocked the little man's escape with his blade – then stick-handled the little fellow back and forth, five times in a row, and none too gently, to prevent him dodging away.

"*Ouch! Ouch!*" shrieked the little man.

"*Be still then!*" ordered Fergus. "Or I'll slap-shoot your right into that black hemlock tree!"

"*Ow! You ferrin devil!*"

"I can keep this up all day, you know!" (It was indeed a fine exhibition of backwoods stick-handling.)

"Agreed! You win!" yelped the little man. "Put up your big hurley stick. For I'm all beat black and blue!"

But before the exhausted little fellow could wiggle away, Fergus had snatched off his own red woollen cap and popped it over the little man, making him his prisoner.

The little man wriggled and spat furiously but could not escape.

"You're mine now!" gloated Fergus. "And the rules say you've got to give me a wish!"

"*Niver the day!*" protested the little fellow. "Where's your lawyer?"

"*Ah now!*" smiled Fergus, for he had heard about the trickery of these wee folk. "Just because I'm an ignorant émigré boy, in a far foreign land, don't believe you can deceive me! I am familiar with the general rules of it all, you know – for didn't my old feller tell me all about the fairies and the secret folk, and how it all was done back in the old green country, and didn't he tell me all the customs of it, from the time I was myself a tiny babe upon his knee!"

"*Niver the day*! Your old dad heard it wrong."

"Not on your nelly, you won't trick me. You owe me three wishes."

"*Three wishes*!" shrieked the little man in outrage. "It was never *three*!"

"Aha! So you admit there *are* wishes involved in the matter, then!"

The little fellow scowled irritably, knowing he had given himself away.

"Alright," he agreed moodily. "But it was never three. Just ...maybe the *one*."

"Ah! My old dad told me you were tricky little folk."

"A sinister libel, entirely!"

"Then give me my rightful three wishes!"

"Never *three. Ouch*! ... But you could maybe have the *one*," said the fairy, trying to negotiate.

"*Three*!" countered Fergus, suddenly tossing the little man onto the ground again and whipping out his hockey stick.

"*Ouch! Ouch*!" shrieked the little man.

"Three wishes! Or into that scratchy hemlock you go!"

"Alright! Alright!" conceded the little man, beaten. "Three small wishes, it is then. Now put away your great thumping shillelagh before you kill the life out of me."

But Fergus still held him fast with his hockey stick.

"On your sworn bond?"

"*Ouch*! Alright! Sworn."

"And you can never go back on your bond, you know," Fergus informed the little man with satisfaction. "For that's a basic rule of the thing, too. A fairy can never go back on his promises, once given."

"You are devilishly well-informed," grumbled the little man, "for a faraway stranger."

"Ah! We youthful émigrés may today be far from the auld sod, but we're still true Irishmen at heart, be we never so far distant over the seas, here in the New World."

"*The New World*!" shrieked the little man in alarm. "Is that where I am, then?"

"Of course, you are," said Fergus in puzzlement. "Didn't you know? You're in Canada."

"*Canada*!" shrieked the little man, even more distraught. "But that's the *cold frozen* part!"

"Well, and where did you think you were going? And come to it, why were you stowed into that freight package in the first place?"

"I was just maybe hitchin' a small ride," said the wee fellow, evasively.

"Why?"

The little man again shifted uneasily.

"*Come along now!*" Fergus threatened.

The little man frowned. Then said reluctantly: "And have you never heard, then, the old rumour that the fairies are departing?"

"I have indeed often heard that rumour," admitted Fergus. "– Indeed, my old feller often recalled that, even when he himself was a boy, the fairies were already all going out of Ireland like mad – but no one knew where they were all going to," mused Fergus. "– And where *did* you all go to?"

"That's for us to know and you to find out," said the little fellow cunningly.

"Well, I know one thing, boyo, you yourself are smartly confined to the penalty box in Barneyville, Upper Canada – and you owe me three of the best, paid on demand."

The little man scowled. "Spit out your wish then, if you must."

"Ah! *Three* wishes, it was! None of your fairy tricks."

The fairy scowled.

"Sure," grumbled the little fellow, "and it'll just be pots of gold again,"

"Not this once," said Fergus. "- But it comes to my mind to ask: how are your good people on the silver?"

***

It was some weeks later, up in the Dominion capital, in the famous town of Ottawa, itself famously situated on a certain mighty northern river, by good fortune and convenience also called *The Ottawa* (and a fine wintry early March morning it was as well) - when a certain prominent Ottawa businessman, Mr. Philip D. Ross, the leading newspaper proprietor of that fine young city, had seated himself in his big leather newspaper office chair, leafing through the morning mail and perusing, for an unusually long time, one particularly puzzling letter. It was an awkward, hand-written letter, traced laboriously on a large foolscap sheet of school writing paper, in a hand that was painfully difficult to decipher — all big capitals and block letters, but in a muzzy misshapen sprawl.

The newspaper proprietor called his Chief Editor.

"Look here, Smirke. What do you make of this?'

"It looks like writing, sir. Some kind of message."

"Well, I know that! But is it in English?"

"I believe so."

And Smirke adjusted his pince-nez and bent closer.

'Deer sors, I take pin and paper in hand to ...'

"Pin?"

"It's something about pins and paper, sir — I believe."

"Pins and paper? Dammit, are we a Stationer's Shop? Who are these people?"

"Ah – wait a moment. I was mistaken…. It seems to be an attempt at correspondence - about the Cup, sir," Smirke ventured at last. "Some rustic fellows wanting to challenge."

"The Cup? The Dominion Bowl?"

"So it seems."

"Well then, why do they want pins and paper?"

"I've no idea, sir."

"But they want to challenge for the Cup?"

"It seems so."

"Let me see that again."

For in that era, Mr. Philip D. Ross, the proprietor of the *Ottawa Evening Journal*, was also, in addition to being guardian of that excellent daily news organ, one of two appointed Trustees for the famous Lord Stanley Silver Cup - responsible for arranging the competition for that mighty converted claret bowl. But in those early days, competed as a purely amateur affair (for all this occurred in a more innocent era, long ago, when there was no serious money in the matter.)

"But who are they?"

"Well, sir, I can make out something here… it appears to be signed by "The Shamrocks".

"Good lord! The *Montreal* Shamrocks?"

"I suppose so."

"But those Montreal fellows only just *lost* the cup a month ago. They gave up the cup to those splendid Winnipeg fellows."

"Well, perhaps they want another go."

"Well they *can't!*"

"And besides," Ross added, "the Shamrocks aren't league champion now. They've lost the title this year. It's our fine Ottawa boys are the eastern champions now. "

"Yes, sir. But as we've just learned, our Ottawa chaps have decided not to challenge these splendid Winnipeg fellows this end of season. They say they are too beat up and injured from their league play, to try to regain the trophy just now."

"Craven fellows,' criticized Ross.

"But perhaps the Montreal Shamrocks want to take up their spot."

"Well they *can't*! These damned Montreal Shamrocks – aren't they're all McGill College fellows and that sort of thing? They should know better."

"Yes," agreed Smirke, "these Montreal people are always difficult. – But wait a moment – here's a postmark?"

"Montreal?"

"No … it looks like … Blarney …? Ah! No, *Barneyville!*"

"*Barneyville*? Where the deuce is Barneyville?"

"No idea. But they do claim to be proper league champions."

"Well, they'd *have* to be, dammit! Only league champions can challenge."

"Well they claim they *are*."

"This is infernally awkward, Smirke. I knew those rules you made up were too loose."

"*I*, sir! But it was you and Sheriff Sweetland who decided what the challenge rules were to be. I merely copied down what you instructed! I protest, sir! I didn't write them!"

"Ah, but to come to the finer point of the matter - and just whose fingerprints and elegant clerk's-hand might be found upon the sole legal copy of the rules? - Should it ever come to a court of the Queen's law?"

"*Sir!*"

But it was no use Smirke's protesting. Jurisprudentially-speaking, Ross had him jammed hard into a tight legal corner – pinned up against the boards and clutched firmly by his suspenders, and with a big legal shinny stick wedged between his knees. (For although this was only 1901, it *was* already Ottawa, after all.)

"The challenge will be accepted then?"

"Well, we must. Those are your rules."

"I shall respond to these bush-league Shamrocks then? And inform the Winnipeg people?"

"Yes. But only after I meet with Sheriff Sweetland, the other Trustee, to set the specific terms. -But it's still your fault."

"*Sir!*"

***

And so it was, only a few late wintry evenings later, that Mr. P.D. Ross and that other much-respected Stanley Cup Trustee, Sheriff John Sweetland, were seated *tête à tête*, in two big, comfortable leather armchairs, close by the fireside of the luxurious Rideau Club, pondering the letter.

"No, no, no," said Sheriff John Sweetland. "It's impossible."

"But yet," frowned Ross, "to be fair, John ... these fellows from Barneyburg *are* the first and only challengers to come forward this end-of-season."

"Our stalwart Ottawa boys have definitely declined?"

"They're too bruised up from the season's tough play. - So they claim."

"Damned pussies," grumbled Sweetland, uncharitably.

"*Are* they?"

"And so," growled Sweetland, "for the moment, this new year end-of-season of 1901 would appear to be the first year, since the Cup competition began, without a challenge offered to the cup holders by some decent city champion?"

"It would."

"Only these rustic Barneyburgers?"

"Just so."

Sweetland rose from his comfortable chair and went to look down from a window, down into a snowy Wellington Street below.

In the darkening avenue below, twilight was descending, and a curtaining snowfall flickered through the dull light of the gas-lamps. A few young women from the government offices were daintily attempting to cross the muddy street, lifting their long skirts and making their way between the carriages and cabs. And nearby, outside a greengrocer's shop, some wee small fellow seemed to be inspecting a few specimens from a barrel of winter spuds.

"Peculiar …Let me see that letter again."

For just then, a strange elfin mist seemed to seep and steal mystically into the elegant Rideau Club, a kind of greenish spell of enchantment and fairy glamour. And for Sheriff John Sweetland, everything now began to seem more softly defined, more dream-like, more magical. Sounds were more hushed and colours more vibrant. More green.

"But yet, on the other hand … d'ye know now…," Sheriff Sweetland slowly began to intone, turned himself rather unaccountably dreamy.

"Yes?"

"- How strange. - For d'you know, just at this moment, I was meself entirely set to oppose this backwoods challenge ... until the just-now, it was … when a strange, new, dewy sort of feeling seemed oddly to steal over and upon myself, entirely."

"Why are you *talking* like that?"

"And further, d'ye know, I can now declare myself to be entirely after-thinkin' that these doughty Barneyburg lads must be the fine, noble, plucky boyos, to the man of them. - And I should be kilt dead entirely, were these fine rustic chaps not to be given their fair and sporting chance at the Cup."

"*What* did you say? Are you unwell?"

Ross stared, wondering himself why he too was now feeling an odd Hibernian turn of phrase arising in himself. He shook himself vigorously.

"We are agreed then that the challenge must be accepted?"

"Well it's certain we must."

"How many matches?"

"Let's just say the one of it. Sure, and we try for more than the one deciding match at this very late season - and wouldn't they all be playin' in a melted thaw puddle by the time? - If you go to that of it."

"Why are you *talking* like that?"

"I can't truly say. My tongue suddenly went all loose and waggly, entirely of itself. Give me a drink."

***

And so it also came about, one early March morning, that Fergus O'Donnell and a wee companion were standing by the ticket window of the CPR wharf and baggage office in the noble hamlet of Barneyville.

"Train tickets for all the boys, is it, Fergus?" inquired old Leonard Dowd, the CPR station agent, waggishly. "And you'll be wantin' to go to Mud Lake to see the girls again, I suppose."

"Not this outing, Len," grinned Fergus. "But all the way to Winnipeg."

"*Winny-peg*!" exclaimed the agent. "Pull another one. Nobody from here ever goes to Winny-peg."

"Well, the Shamrocks are goin'!" said Fergus stoutly. "The boys are goin' to play for the Cup!"

"*No!*" Old Len nodded knowingly. Then reflecting deeply for a long moment, he added: "And what 'Cup' might that be, then, Fergus?"

"The great famous silver punch bowl himself," said Fergus. "The Lord Stanley's Cup."

"Can't say as I've ever heard of that feller," agreed Len. "Not local then, I suppose."

And he leaned out from his wicket and looked curiously down at the small fellow standing beside Fergus's left knee – odd little chap.

"But you fellows can't get all the way to Winny-peg by the old lake steamer, boy. The old *John A.* doesn't like to paddle so far west as all that," the agent said. "You'll have to take her down to Port Pickerel at the end of Lake Witchigichi. Then you'd need to catch the CPR train west, via Ottawa, the Nation's Capital."

"That's what I want, then. Rail tickets for the boys, all through to Winnipeg and return."

"And via Ottawa, the Nation's Capital then, is it?"

"Is there another train route westward?"

"Not that I know of."

"That's what we'll have then."

And bending down to the wee fellow, his companion, Fergus whispered:

"And don't forget all the boys get full expenses and *per diems* too," said Fergus, "for that was part of the one first wish as well."

"*One wish*, you'd call that!"

"It was one of those omnibus wishes," agreed Fergus.

"Bejesus! And you'll be the ruin of me!" complained the little fellow.

"And just how far distant is this Winnipeg town?" now demanded the wee small fellow, clambering up and taking out a tiny notebook and making some anxious financial calculations.

"Well now. Seems ... hardly no more than 1200 miles, roughly-speaking," informed Len, consulting his big schedule book. "Four days only. - Collisions permitting."

"*What!*" shrieked the little fellow, looking in shock at the cost of the Fares and Tariffs.

"Four days, *provisional*, that is," cautioned Len, in his official agent's capacity. "Excepting usual rail accidents and boiler explosions over the Lakehead - 'for which the CPR railroad company assumes no legal responsibility'."

"And *Return*, don't forget," reminded Fergus. "Fares and *per diems* for 8 players – all the boys."

"*Eight!* You said you were the Barneyville *Seven!*"

"Seven and a Spare," corrected Fergus. "That's the usual way of it. - And don't forget, I've yet got two more wishes still comin' to me. - And don't overlook the boxed lunches for the journey."

"I'll be bankrupt sure entire," groaned the little man. "And I suppose next you'll be wishing me to fix the match."

Fergus was mortally shocked.

"Most certainly *not!*" exclaimed Fergus. "A fair sporting chance is all that any true-hearted shinny player asks. Put the Barneyville boys on the frozen pond with these grand famous Winnipeg fellers, and we'll ask no more," said Fergus with some heat.

– For was not the very club motto of the Shamrocks: *Manly Purity and Fair Play*? - And a grand, noble motto that motto was indeed, such as any young hero would be proud to skate out under, into battle – and a resplendent motto also, beautifully stitched in silk threads upon a refined green and gold team banner – most delicately embroidered there by the maidenly fingers of several admiring and rather well-figured younger ladies of the local branch of the Imperial Order of the Daughters of the Empire.

"So that's eight by rail and return, then?" confirmed the agent.

"And one additional child, please," added Fergus, nodding down at his wee companion. "Half-fare."

A wee splutter of outrage came from below.

"*Child*, is it?" asked Len doubtfully, leaning out of his wicket and peering down again to inspect the wee fellow. "And how old is the little feller?"

"Five hund ...," the little man started to blurt out.

"He's just five," said Fergus.

"Well, I'd say the little feller's kind of scrunched up and wrinkly for a mere lad of five," ventured the agent, suspiciously. "You're not tryin' to come 'round me, then?"

"*Ah!* you're too many for me today, Len," Fergus agreed amiably. "To be truthful: he's five and bit more besides."

"And he's what, d'ye say?"

"From the old country."

"Ah! That would explain it, then. Poor half-famished little tyke."

"That's it," agreed Fergus. "So just punch out those tickets, and he'll be paying."

"*He'll* be paying? The wee little feller of five?"

"It's his shout."

"*Well indeed!*" Len exclaimed, pushing back his old blue cap and scratching his head wonderingly. "- And at the first sight of him, I would have said: *there's* a wee feller, that there would likely be no money at all in his pocket!"

"He has a small magical purse though," said Fergus.

"Ah, so that would be it, then."

***

It was some days later, and some miles beyond the top of Lake Superior, that a darkened, smoke-begrimed Canadian Pacific Railway steam locomotive engine, with a long line of wooden railway carriages attached, sat dead still and silent, shunted into a remote siding just off the main line westward. Dead parked and unmoving, as that westbound train had been now for nearly 16 hours.

Inside one of the cramped and unheated wooden carriages, the fine, noble boys from Barneyville were not happy.

"Bejesus! I'm freezing!" complained Tommy Hankin, shivering despite his muffler and his heavy, hand-knitted woollen sweater – the traditional Canadian one with a lumpy brown moose and a bunch of green pine trees worked into it. (His Granny had knitted it up from an Eaton's mail-order catalogue pattern, as a Christmas present for her favourite boy, in '97.) "Is there never to be any heat in this thing?"

"Next stop, Arctic Circle," grumbled Rory Burn, peering out a frosted window

Outside, the dark and barren wilderness howled with northern wind and flurries of snow – and not a light, nor a heavenly star in sight, in the dark clouded sky. Somewhere in the distance, wolves also howled in pain, into the black night.

"Just a short delay, lads," said the affable Conductor, as he passed down the narrow aisle with a coal-oil lantern, squeezing between the hard, wooden and slatted benches that served for seats to a trainload of huddled, westbound emigrants.

"*Short* delay, is it! And you've been saying that for a day and a night now, while we've been sittin' here freezin' in the dark!"

"Well now, the railroad's got itself a small accident up ahead on the line, boys. Just a dozen cars gone off the tracks – but, god be praised, hardly anybody kilt on this onc."

"When can we get moving again?"

"Well, lookin' to the bright positive side, the wrecking train and crew from Rat Portage should be coming through any time now, to clear the line. And then we should get the signal to get back onto the main line and happily on yer road again."

"Happily!" fretted Fergus O'Donnell. "The team's got to be in Winnipeg before the tenth of March, or we forfeit the match!"

"Plenty of time, boys. Lots of time."

"*The boys of Barneyville are going to remember this one, Fergus O'Donnell!*" an aggrieved voice called out in the darkness.

"Yes, the glory of the Cup, you said. – And where's all the extra ham sandwiches gone?"

For, sad to say, the Barneyville Seven (plus the one Spare) had been quarrelling and bickering for several days now. Team morale was not high. The trouble had started, it seems, when the boys first discovered that instead of being booked on a plush, fancy passenger train westward, the tickets Fergus had in his pocket were for second-class wooden benches in an elderly westbound emigrant car, filled with huddled fathers, mothers and crying children.

"You got the boxed lunches, didn't you?"

"We ate all those two days ago. And now we're starving."

"Yes, and how can we play this grand famous match if we're all shrivelled up and weak from hunger?"

"*I wish I'd never come!*" wailed a voice.

Things were not going so well, it seems.

"And where's that sneaky little feller – your cousin?"

"Yes! Ask Shorty where the extra ham sandwiches went!"

"Yes, for isn't it likely that that wee feller, Shorty Fay, ate them all himself!" accused another indignant voice.

"Not long to wait now, boys," said the Conductor cheerily, coming back into the car. "Telegraph line says the repair crew might be starting out Sunday morning, right after church."

"This is a disaster!" Bartel Clancy moaned. "And don't I wish all this had never happened!"

Fergus fumbled his way back to the Second Baggage Car, to check again anxiously on the safety of the team equipment –a pile of battered hockey sticks and a heap of skates.

There he found the wee small fellow, drawn up cosily beside a blazing pot-bellied wood stove, seated on a half-keg of galvanized nails - trying a few rounds of Two-Handed Euchre with the Baggage Guard.

"I niver had such bleedin' bad luck at cards in my life," complained the Guard, "I just can't fathom it."

The wee little fellow quickly covered up a large collection of nickels and dimes.

"You'd think he had cards up his sleeve," the Guard grumbled. "But he don't."

"This is a disaster," Fergus whispered to the little man. "The Shamrocks have got to get to Winnipeg by the Tuesday or forfeit the match."

"Ah. You'd certainly be wantin' to spend your last wish then," the wee little man nodded craftily, concealing his playing cards.

"*Now*! - It's the *two* wishes still remaining to me, not just the one!" Fergus corrected sharply.

The little fellow scowled.

"I wonder," asked the Guard, searching through his empty pockets, "could some kind soul be lending me four-bits - or a dollar? I appear to be cleaned out."

"At four?" asked the wee fellow.

"*Four*! It was only three percent before!"

"Sure, and didn't we recently cross over some Time Zone, you said?

"Well … yes. She goes into Central Clock Time after Dryden," agreed the baffled guard. "So your rate goes up?"

"Farther from Greenwich."

"What?"

"Currency has to travel farther. Additional rail charges."

"Oh...," nodded the guard, scratching his head and looking puzzled. "Sterling money, is it? ...Well then, if that's the case ... "

He looked hard at his cards for a moment.

"So, I'll have only the four-bits for the present, and we'll just try a few more hands at the cards?"

"Sure, and that would be only fairness itself," agreed the wee fellow. "Just sign here."

***

It was finally two days later, after one last, brief, unexplained halt at some lonely junction, to unhitch some extra cars, that an ice-shrouded CPR steam train chugged its slow way across the Manitoba border, finally puffing its way into the noble town of Winnipeg, at mid-morning light.

"Here she be, boys," announced the affable Conductor, as the train creaked into the icy station. "Famed golden gateway to the West. And right on schedule, as usual."

"On schedule!" protested Fergus, rubbing frost off a window to catch a glimpse of the smoky metropolis.

"– *Attention, all youse foreign people!*" the Conductor suddenly shouted at an uncomprehending immigrant crowd, now milling in confusion in the aisle beside their wooden seats. "*Everybody get out! -Last stop!*"

Then the Conductor added: "*And the C.P.R. railroad company wishes youse all a pleasant stop-over, before continuing on your ways to Saskatchewan. Connecting westbound train now standing on Platform 4, departing in 4 minutes! - Hurry up there, missus.*"

"And you mind your steps there too, sonny," he further warned as he flung open the heavy car door onto the snow-filled platform; and then half-pitched some furry-wrapped little fellow out the door and into wintry Winnipeg.

"*Ye great lummoxy idjiot!*" protested the wee small fellow, picking himself up out of the snow.

"*Jeez!*" whistled the startled Conductor in astonishment, turning to a young mother and baby, who were also lined up to exit. "And did'ya ever hear a mouth like that? - and on such a small item of a child?"

But soon the Barneyville Seven themselves (plus one Spare) were also jostled down the steps from their chilly passenger carriage and into the snow, followed by a crush of escaping emigrants, who had already heard the warning whistle of their connecting train, about to depart. They rushed off blindly in search of Platform 4 for Saskatchewan.

Then the mighty Shamrocks were left alone, assembling themselves on the snow-drifted train platform of the half-buried CPR station, their collective breaths steaming into the frozen air.

"Right then," suggested Fergus, taking charge, "and how would it be, Tim Leary, were you yourself to stay here to collect all the sticks and skates, when they come off the Second Baggage Car? Meanwhile, the rest of the boys and myself will scout down that direction, for wherever this Winnipeg shinny pond might be at."

"And it's all *myself alone,* you're sayin', Fergus O'Donnell," protested young Tim Leary, "who has to hump all the equipment over to this famous Winny-peg rink? - if ever you might find the thing?"

"And aren't you the Spare, then?" noted Fergus.

"And what's in that?" young Tim Leary demanded heatedly.

"Everybody knows the spare man always humps the equipment on a famous road trip. This is the immortal Cup itself we'll be playin' for today, don't you know that, young Tim Leary? Starting Seven, the veterans, need to preserve their manly vigour for the match itself."

"I never heard about any famous road trip rule before!" grumbled young Leary.

"That's because Barneyville's never *been* on a famous road trip before," observed Tommy Hankin.

"What about...? "started to challenge Bartel Clancy.

"That was local, only."

"Boys, this is the grand, famous western metropolis of the whole nation, Winnipeg, Province of Manitoba, not Stumptville. A different level of sophistication and skilled play, entirely. These Winnipeg boys are legends."

"Yes, it's gathered for a high purpose, we are, young Leary."

"Too true!" added Bartel Clancy. "The Shamrocks are in the big time now, young Tim, soon to be desperately and hopelessly playin' out our mortal lives for the famous Lord Stanley's silver Cup. The starting Seven need to preserve all their manly fluids for the match."

"So just fetch the shinny gear along, young Tim, and hump it over to the playing rink -wherever that might be."

"Why doesn't the wee small fella do it? He isn't playin'."

"And neither will you be, if you don't fetch up the team's sticks and skates."

"You're gettin' a bit big for your galoshes, Fergus O'Donnell."

"And who was it then, got up this famous match in the first place?"

"I thought it must have been this little feller, your cousin. He's a small wee fella, but he seems to have all the brains in the family. – And by the way, how did Shorty come to acquire that big warm fur coat, when we're all just freezin' in our grannies' wool sweaters?"

(The unity of the Barneyville Seven plus one Spare was still a bit frayed, after their long train journey west.)

"If you care to step outside and say those words again, Tim Leary."

"We *are* outside. And I'm still freezin'! So where's this famous rink?"

"It must be around here somewhere, near the town. So let's stop fighting for the puck and get this match on the ice, boys."

"Right!" agreed Tommy Hankin. "First order of business for the House: find this Winnipeg shinny pond."

So, in the end, Tim Leary grumpily did stay behind, waiting for the Second Baggage Car to be unloaded, while the veteran Shamrocks wandered away from the station, searching vaguely for the famous Winnipeg pond.

"She'll be down that way, no doubt," said Michael Davies, nodding at some large, frozen river off in the lower distance, winding through the flats below old fur trading town.

"And what noble stream might that be, then?" asked Larry Rooney.

"That would be the deep mystery to me," shrugged Michael Davies. "But I don't see any other likely spot."

They trudged on, to get a closer view of the frozen river.

"Well, the thing does indeed seem big enough for a decent playing surface," said Rory Burn, nodding at the windings and snowy bends of the big river down the slope.

"Agreed. These Winnipeg boys could easily fit in a regulation ice-surface or two, if the current's not too strong."

"We'll go down that way, then, and have a look," said Fergus. "But I still don't see any rink."

"Probably their town pond's just around that bend down there," offered Tommy Hankin. "It's a lee shore."

"That'd be smart," nodded Owen Smithers. "For the wind's out here's something ferocious."

"They are well-known to be smart people out here, these Winnipeggers," Fergus agreed. "So it stands to reason they'd put their pond down in some sheltered bend."

"Lee shore," repeated Tommy Hankin, sagely.

"We'll look down that way then."

But when the Shamrocks had trudged closer to the stream and had slogged through waist-high snow to the icy riverside, and when they had further trudged a hundred yards along the shore to the first sheltering curve of the river, there was still no sign of any Winnipeg shinny pond.

"Where the devil did they put the cursed thing, then?" asked Emmett Leary, scratching his head. For nowhere in sight was the celebrated Winnipeg ice-rink, home of the current Stanley Cup Champions.

Fergus scanned the icy width of the frozen stream. Far out on the frozen river he sighted an old fellow ice-fishing, seated upon a broken kitchen chair - an old boy with a warm Tam 'O Shanter tugged down over his ears and a thick tartan shawl wrapped over his shoulders,

"We'll go out and ask that old Scottish feller," decided Fergus. "He'd likely be local."

The boys trudged out across the hard ice of the river.

"Pardon there, good sir," called out Fergus to the old gentleman. "And could you be tellin' us visitors, where-at's the famous Winnipeg ice-rink? We can't seem to be finding the thing."

"Och, ice rink, is it now?" questioned the old fellow, wiping snow from his beard.

"Yessir."

"Ice rink, you'd be inquiring for? For the Curling?"

"No, the shinny."

"Ah! For the Ice-hockey then."

"Yessir. That's the one."

"Och, well it's never down here that you'll find it, laddies."

And the old fellow went back to checking his fishing line.

Fergus paused. "But would you happen to know where it *would* be, then?"

"Where *what* would be?"

"The famous Winnipeg Ice Rink – We're just askin' after its location – the general whereabouts where our fellas might be locating the thing? - As we're after playin' an important championship match this afternoon, against your Winnipeg fellows – and the time is getting urgent."

"Well, laddie, it's not down here, you know. This down here would be just the River, not the Auditorium."

"The Auditorium?"

"I just related that – the Auditorium."

Fergus was confused. "I don't know ..."

"Wait, wait, let's pause the conversation a moment. - Aren't you the laddies who were just now lookin' to play some shinny?"

"Well, yes. We're here to play for the famous Cup."

"A hockey Cup, would that be? Not the Curling?"

"Yes. In fact, the Lord Stanley's Cup. We're Barneyville."

"Never heard of Barneyville. But if its playin' the hockey you're seeking out, it's never down here. Ice-fishing, yes, but not the ice-hockey. This is the River, not the Auditorium."

"The ...?"

"The *Auditorium*. – Are you not listening, laddie? It's back up that way, up at Garry. - No, up that other way. Look for the big building."

"A *building*?"

"You're wantin' some ice-*hockey*? Not the ice-*fishin*'?"

"Yes, that would be the way of it, because ..."

"Nor the Curling?"

"No."

"Then you'll want to find the *Auditorium*. I thought I just said that? Go back up towards town there."

"Wait a moment, here. You'd be tellin' us, then, that people out here play shinny *in a building*? - Not on a proper outdoors pond?"

"Certainly. Of course."

Fergus and the Barneyville boys stood stunned.

"He's pullin' your leg," whispered Michael Davies

"Who ever heard of playin' shinny inside a *building*!" added Owen Smithers.

"Seriously, sir ...." smiled Fergus.

But the old fellow paid no more attention.

"We'd best go back up the hill and look."

At this, there was a general complaining of the boys.

"Bedad," also grumbled the wee small fellow, up to his wee neck in a snow drift. "And don't I wish that I'd never come this way in the first instance. I could have stowed to Australia!!"

"Aha!" said Fergus cunningly. "Is *that* where the Fairies departed to, then?"

"Niver you mind!" the little man said hastily, looking rather anxious.

The boys had no choice but to trudge all the way back up the slope again. But eventually, by luck, they stumbled across what seemed to be a more promising locale, where they discovered buildings and some broad streets.

"Well, she's a *big place*, this town, isn't she?" calculated Rory Burn, nervously admiring the wide streets and tall commercial buildings of the famed western metropolis.

"This would be high-level living, boys! Look at that Department Store!"

"Bejesus! And they've got *two Banks*!" said Emmett Leary. "Right on the same street!"

"There's money here, boys," said Tommy Hankin, "that's for certain."

And all the Shamrock Seven felt an uneasy nervousness and discomfort, feeling their own lack of sophistication in this glamorous, worldly place. And some of them, for the first time, began to secretly feel that they were perhaps getting in over their heads, skilled shinny or no.

"Come, brace up, boys," said Fergus nervously. "We'll be just grand when we're on the ice."

"*Shamrocks Forever!*" chimed in all the boys. But not so confidently as when still back at home.

"Look there – might that be something relevant? - Up that direction, in the distance up ahead? - that big cow-barny thing - that enormous wooden shed up that street, then?" asked Owen Smithers, pointing at a large edifice looming off in the distance.

"It might be that."

"Excuse me, sir," Fergus called out to a passing gentleman wrapped in a large fur coat. "We are out-of-town visitors, seeking to locate the famed Winnipeg shinny rink."

"The shinny rink?"

"That would be it."

"Not the curling rink?"

"No, the shinny. For the ice hockey."

"Well, you're looking right at it, son," said the man, hurrying on.

The Shamrocks all stared in awe at the enormous barnlike building up ahead.

"I suppose that could be it, then," whispered Tommy Hankin.

The boys moved warily closer, in some confusion.

"Ah, it *is* that," said Michael Davies, taking off his spectacles to peer up at a sign out front, that clearly stated, in big white-painted letters: *AUDITORIUM*.

And at that confirmation, all the boys stepped nervously back a pace or two, uncertain and not quite knowing what to do.

"Well ..." said Fergus slowly, "I suppose we might just take a peek inside. To be sure, then, that this *is* the right place."

"Well, it *says* it's the place."

"Well, we can't know that for certain, just because it says so on that board."

"We'll just peek inside then?"

"I suppose we'd best."

But they all stood still for several minutes longer, nervously, as an arctic wind gusted and chewed its way down the street.

"*Bejesus,*" complained the wee small fellow, "and will ye just be standing and gawking like backwoods idjiots, the whole of this windy winter noon-hour, then? Let's get inside, where there's perhaps some *heat* to be had!"

"Your small cousin's getting' cranky."

"And aren't we all, then?" complained Tommy Hankin. "For in my own judgment, this is the worst famous road trip the Shamrocks have ever taken!"

"The *only* famous road trip, it is," corrected Owen Smithers.

"Just that," agreed Bartel Darcy.

"But what about ..."

"Now, boys!" cut in Fergus. "*Shamrocks Forever!*"

At that reminder, the boys were chastened, and looked down guiltily at their nailed boots.

"So we'll just go inside then. All agreed?"

It was not long before the doughty Shamrock Seven were staring in awe at a gleaming indoor ice surface, surrounded by a low rail, and standing places for many, many spectators.

"*Bejesus!*" whistled Owen Smithers in awe. "Who could have thought? These Winnipeggers have indeed put their shinny rink *right indoors of a building* – and *right in the very middle of the place as well!*"

"On the other hand," Tommy Hankin suggested, "it might be that they *afterward* put a building up, around their outdoor shinny rink, - To cut down on the wind."

"It could well be either," adjudicated Michael Davies, "us not knowing the actual history of the thing. - But the important fact is – there it is!"

"*And here we are!*" said an awed voice. "The Barneyville boys! To be playing for the famous celebrated Silver Cup!"

"*Just to think of it!*" gasped someone else, breathlessly. "And it might be, that at this very same moment in time, somewhere, secretly hidden, yet very close at hand … and right the inside of this very Winnipeg Auditorium of it … that the Governor-General's grand glorious and famous silver bowl could be possibly sittin' here *right now*, bein' entirely itself!"

"No! *The Lord Stanley's silver cup,* you're meaning?"

"You think it's really right here? Right now?"

"Where else? And aren't these splendid Winnipeg fellows the current Champions?"

"Maybe they keep it in a safety vault … one of those banks we saw," put in Tommy Hankin.

"Don't be daft. For if you had the thing, wouldn't you want it along with you, where everybody could see it?"

"Somebody might want to steal it."

"*Niver*! God Himself would strike them dead!"

"You believe?"

"Certainly. This is the Lord Stanley's *Cup*, man! Not just some silvery church treasure from the Vatican, or that sort of thing."

"I suppose you're right in that," all the boys agreed.

And a fearful, sacred hush now fell upon the Barneyville boys, as they gazed awe-struck around the lighted interior of the legendary Winnipeg Auditorium, home of those god-like heroes, the Winnipeg *Victorias*, the seven most sublime shinny players in all the created cosmos (plus one Spare). For now the rustic Barneyville boys truly believed that somewhere in the hushed, sacred hollow of that big barnlike auditorium, silently and spiritually radiating itself - and at that very moment in earthly time as well– lay the numinous Lord Stanley's Grail itself!

"Besides, it would have to be here today," Fergus added, "in case the Shamrocks should accidentally happen to win the match."

It was then that the noble Shamrocks felt an even colder, deadlier shiver, a thrill of manly dread run down their backs – the shiver of scary reality. *The grand match was for real!*

"Bejesus! And don't I feel some sickly!" Tommy Hankin suddenly announced, staggering a bit in the legs

And likewise, all the Barneyville Seven were suddenly white-faced and more than a bit unsteady.

(The only one not so awed was the wee small fellow, who was busily toting up some alarming financial figures in his wee accounts ledger.)

Nervously, and in even greater awe, the boys again looked around, more in dread than hope – and for the first time noticed an early straggle of Winnipeg spectator-folk, already seeping into the place and making their way to rink-side, for game time was close at hand.

So the great adventure *was* indeed actually about to begin! Within a few short tickings of mortal time, the now very scared, but still doughty lads from backwoods Barneyville would be skating out onto this misty alien ice surface, to challenge the hometown Cup champions for the great silver Grail!

"And would there be anything stiff and handy to drink about here?" whispered Owen Smithers, rather ghastly-faced. "Do you suppose?"

But at that moment, a manly baritone voice called out a greeting:

"Hello, *you fellows*! You're the Shamrocks. Welcome. You've made it just in time."

Before them appeared a sturdy, muscular Winnipeg player, already uniformed and kitted out in his skates and hockey gear – and sporting on the breast of his wool sweater the celebrated red buffalo crest of the champion, godlike, divine, ultra-human, legendary Winnipeg *Victorias*, the Lord Stanley's Cup defenders of 1901!

"I'm Bain," greeted the sturdy Winnipeg captain, shaking hands all around. "Our fellows were just about to take our warm-up. Your lads can have the ice next, whenever you're equipped and ready."

The Shamrocks gaped in awe.

"Bejesus, it's *Bain*!" whispered Michael Davies, in a tone of reverence.

"And who's he then? When he's at home?" whispered Tommy Hankin.

"You great idjiot! He's only the Captain of the Cup Champions and top man on the team!"

"No!" whispered Tommy Hankin.

"Let me introduce your fine chaps to our own fellows," Dan Bain said, leaning courteously on his hockey stick. "This is Gingras, then Brown next, Johnson and Wood over there, and these two hearties are the Fletts."

For now the other six sturdy Winnipeg *Victorias* had gathered around, to cast amiable but steely glances over the poor Barneyville squad, piercingly sizing each of them up, despite the half-smiles of courtesy.

"It's straight to business with these lads, no nonsense," whispered Michael Davies to Emmett Leary, uncomfortably.

"And your fellows?"

"We would be… Barneyville," was all that a tongue-tied Fergus O'Donnell could utter.

The famous Dan Bain, centreman of the champion *Victorias*, gave a quizzical look.

"Well …excellent!. Our chaps will go out and have our warm-up first then, while you fellows get your gear on? Agreed?"

"Grand," agreed Fergus.

"Stout fellows! And shall we say, start of match in … oh, about one-ish or so? Will that be agreeable?"

"First rate," agreed Fergus.

"*Topping*! Our fellows will go out first then!"

"Grand."

"Tally ho!"

"Topping."

And with that, the great Bain flashed out onto the ice surface, then flashed around the rink at rocketing speed, weaving and dodging imaginary opponents, with thrilling muscularity, grace, and skill.

"Oh dear," said Owen Smithers.

"We're in for it now," groaned Bartel Darcy

"We'll be drubbed, sure," somebody else mumbled.

The Barneyville boys now watched as the other six famous *Victorias* also took dynamically to the ice, dashing mightily about the rink, the rubber zipping from man to man at break-neck speed.

"And it's some *really* bad I'm feeling now," gasped Tommy Hankin. "Not just sickly."

"Let's go home," whispered Owen Smithers.

"Gather your legs under you, boys!" Fergus urged, a little weakly. "*Stand firm, the Shamrocks!*"

"*I wish we'd never come!*"

"Courage, boys!" rallied Emmett Leary. "Onward to glory, the Barneyville boys! Shinny gear and weapons at the ready!"

"And just where *is* our shinny gear?" now asked Michael Davies, peering around over his spectacles. "For I myself don't see our trusty gear or weapons anywhere about. Do you boys?"

"There's a good point now."

"Young Tim Leary's fetching them, I suppose."

"But where *is* young Tim?"

"Bejesus, he can't still be back at the train station."

But just then young Tim Leary stomped in, very irritably, and covered head to foot in ice and snow, and looking none too pleased.

"*Grand!* - And you couldn't send out a scout, to tell me where you boys were at, then?"

He shook the snow from his mackinaw coat.

"And it's to be orphaned and abandoned in the wilderness of Winnipeg, Manitoba, that I am, is it? And not a friendly face to guide me!" he said accusingly to his big brother, Emmett.

Fergus and the other Six frowned guiltily. "Sorry, young Tim. We forgot. In the excitement of it all."

"*Forgot*, was it! And me left to hump the shinny gear up and down snowbanks and icy riverbanks – while you're all warm inside, pleasuring yourselves."

"And why couldn't you just have enquired of some local inhabitant then, as did ourselves?" countered Tommy Hankin, rather irritated by criticism of the noble Seven and their manly honour.

"And didn't I do just that? And didn't they just keep sending me to the curling rink?"

"Ah," said Michael. "That was the way of it for you too, was it? But never mind. You've found your way here now."

"Yes," said Bartel Clancy, "and despite all, aren't you here now in the flesh, and isn't that the main concern? - And by the way: where's our gear?"

Young Tim Leary paused.

"Ah… Now there's the problem of it."

"What? You didn't hump over the gear yet, then?" asked Fergus in astonishment.

"Not as such," explained young Tim, reluctantly. "As there isn't any gear."

"*What?*"

"It's gone south."

"South?"

"Exactly so.'

"What do you mean?"

"Well, as Himself, our grand leader here, and some of you lesser beings may recall - and wasn't there one last brief halt at some desolate rail junction on the way in? - But perhaps you dis-remember that small incident?"

"Well …perhaps we might … somewhat," the boys said tentatively.

"It would be good if you had. Because it was at that forlorn junction that our shinny gear went south."

"*Niver!*" said the boys. "… What?"

"Yes. For it was at that identical small rail halt, it seems, that the Second Baggage Car was entirely uncoupled and hitched up to an entirely different train, going south - in the direct manner of speaking."

"*No!* You mean …?"

"Exactly. Some brilliant brain of the expedition seems to have stowed all our shinny gear onto the wrong baggage car, when we climbed aboard in Ottawa, the nation's Capital."

"*Oh no*! But where's our skates and sticks gone to then?"

Young Tim Leary just smiled and hummed a few well-known bars of an anthem.

"*What*! *No*! - Gone south over the American border, is it! Side-switched into the *USA*, you're sayin'?"

"That would seem to be the basic matter of it. It seems the Yankee border is just to the south of here, they'd be tellin' me."

"*No!* Who could have known that? – and away out here in the far west?"

"But how are we going to get our gear back?"

"Emergency Motion to the House!" quickly suggested Tommy Hankin. "I move that the first thing to do, is to discover what exact, particular American States might be currently lying just southward of this general broad geographical area."

"*Bejesus!* And what difference does *that* make," shouted Fergus, "which particular American state our gear's gone to! It's gone!"

"Well," explained Tommy softly, rather hurt, "if you were wantin' to locate your own shinny stick and skates again."

"He's got a point there, Fergus."

"Yes, a fellow would first need to narrow down which particular states to hunt through, not just rush off blind. - Michael, as you're the schoolmaster?"

"Ah, that would again be the hidden mystery to myself," admitted Michael Davies. "As we rarely come to that part of the geography book in Barneyville."

"Might it be California, perhaps?" offered Owen Smithers, hoping to narrow the problem.

"Or Oregon?" suggested Rory Burn. "That's a western state, is it not?"

"Both guesses would seem reasonable," agreed Michael Davies, "as those two States do indeed lie south of our Canadian border, I believe."

"*All* American states lie south of our Canadian border."

"Is that a fact now?"

"Alaska too, then?"

"*Ah*! - Now that *might* be the exception. I'll look that up sometime."

"*Boys!*" Fergus cut in. "*Bejesus! Never mind which Americans states it is!* The question is, how are we going to get our equipment back?"

"Fergus, be reasonable. First things first. - Tim?"

"Well, as I now recollect it," mused young Tim Leary, "the CPR feller *did* say the name of the place. - But then again, I wasn't really listening."

"Not California, then?"

"Not as I now recollect it."

"*But how are we going to get our gear back*!" Fergus persisted.

"Well, Fergus, if you continue in this impatient way, probably we're *not*," advised Michael Davies sagely. "Not if you don't let us work out which U.S. states the gear's possibly gone to, now could we?"

"That's only rational, Fergus."

"Although, in any event," Michael Davies added, "it's perhaps too late for young Tim to hike all the way down there to America and fetch back our shinny gear, as the match itself is about to start in twenty minutes."

"*What?*" protested young Tim heatedly. "And it's again *me myself alone* that has to go all the way down to California and hump back the lost skates and sticks?"

"Young Tim's got a fair point," someone said.

"But what I want to know," said Tommy Hankin irritably, "is who the divil put our shinny gear into the wrong baggage car in the first place."

"Aha! Now you're comin' to it, Sherlock!"

"Not young Tim Leary then?"

"No. For didn't our great leader Fergus O'Donnell delegate a certain small somebody to be the trusty equipment manager?"

"The wee small little fellow, was it, you're suggesting? Shorty Fay, was it then, did the dirty deed?"

"*Grand!*" exclaimed young Tim Leary sarcastically. "So just this once you won't be putting all the slander on myself!"

"And where *is* that wee sneaky little fellow now, for the matter of it?"

The Shamrocks looked around – and noticed that the wee small fellow had conveniently sloped off with himself - and disappeared.

"Aha! And isn't it clear that the guilty conscience is indeed on *him,* the wee small little feller!"

"*Trusty equipment manager!*" criticized Emmet Leary. "Now see what comes of bringing in your own family relatives for the big, soft jobs!"

"Heads up! For the deeper matter of it, where *is* Fergus himself, now?" noted Michael Davies, looking around at the group.

For indeed, Fergus had now also slipped away from the group. - For had not Fergus himself, a moment prior, espied the wee small fellow legging it rapidly towards the rink exit?

"*Devil mend you!*" cried Fergus, catching the wee fellow by the fur coat. "You tricksy little fairy!"

"*Niver the day! A low slander, entirely!*" protested the wee small fellow, in a rather aggrieved, theatrical tone. "And how was I myself to be knowing which of your ferrin devilish railroad cars was to be an *American -bound* baggage car, and myself not local?"

Fergus could only sputter and protest.

"And I'll put it to you further now," protested the wee small fellow, adding a self-righteous finish, "for could any civilized person tell the difference between your own local customs and appearances, and those of the heathen Americans southwards? - For don't you all look *exactly alike* to all the rest of us in the world!"

"*Alike!*"

"And do you think the whole world's supposed to know your own local details and differences, is it?"

"But what are we going to do? Fergus asked desperately.

The wee small fellow looked crafty.

"Well now, and isn't there's yet the last unexpired magical wish in your pocket?"

"*Ah now*! *Two* more wishes remaining, it is!"

The little fellow scowled.

"*Very well then!*" ordered Fergus determinedly, looking the wee fellow sharply in the eye. "Hike off on your fairy nag and fetch back all our skates and sticks, *instanter*! – That would be my second wish! And no time to lose with it!"

The wee small fellow frowned, as if pondering the practicality of this wish.

"Sure, and that wish would be reasonable enough," agreed the wee small fellow, "but for two small difficulties in the actual doing of it."

"*What? What two things?* Is this more trickery?"

"Well in the first place, I'd be needin' a stalk of ragwort for the fairy nag."

"Ragwort?"

"That's the usual way of it, although some fresh cabbage stalk could serve."

"But it's *winter time!*"

"Ah, and so it is then. -And there's the initial problem to it all. No fairy horses at hand."

"*But do you people have no other means of transport? – in an emergency?*"

"Well, it's sometimes possible. But that would then bring us to the second question of difficulty."

"What?"

"Where-at exactly should I be now locating these lost shinny-playing articles? *'Somewhere over the border in America'* is a bit vague, is it not?"

Fergus was momentarily thrown by that.

"But I though fairies ..."

"I'd be needing a good reliable military compass and the map coordinates," said the wee small fellow, thoughtfully. "This being a new and foreign continent to myself, entirely - and myself not yet knowing my way around."

"We *know very well where they've gone to*! They'll be in ..."

Fergus stopped in confusion.

"Ah, now. And it seems you yourself don't actually know the new location either?"

"No, no, wait ... it would be ... no, w*ait, wait!"* Fergus cried desperately.

"It seems your second wish has been just blown off uselessly into the breeze, as you're not knowing the mailing address yourself."

"No, wait! Change that! Revision of the previous second wish!"

"That's not our usual policy."

"No! No! The same second wish, only revised a small wee bit! Just ... re-imagined! Re-purposed! I had my fingers crossed the first time!"

"And you'd be claiming fairies are the tricky folk!"

"So this would still be only my *second* wish, sworn?"

The Fairy sighed.

"And a fairy can never go back on his ...'"

"Bejesus! Just get on with it, man!"

For the small wee little fellow was becoming mightily weary of his unfortunate adventure in the New World.

"*Agreed then*! Revised second wish only!" Fergus cried in a kind of urgent and harried frenzy of decision! "Second wish still – mind it! – is this: fetch us *bran-new skates and sticks,* entirely - not the old ones - strike that part -and for the whole of the boys, mind you, don't try to come around me on that! Spare man included."

"Agree …" the wee little fellow started to say quickly.

"*Wait! Addendum*! And they have to actually fit the boys' feet. *And* they have to be here for the *very start* of the match in twenty minutes! No more tricks!"

The little fellow scowled.

"So it will just be the new ice skates and hockey sticks then?"

But just now Michael Davies rushed in.

"Fergus! What are we to do? The match is about to start! The *Victorias* and the time-keepers are on the ice!"

Fergus had no more time to dither. So he now took unhesitating and decisive command, demonstrating why he was the rightful captain for the team.

"Alright! Fetch us those bran-new ice-skates and hockey sticks, all round!"

"But how can Shorty hump all the way to California and back so fast?" asked Michael Davies, in puzzlement, not understanding what was going on.

But Fergus cut him off. "*Go, get on your nag, you tricky little fairy!*"

The wee small little fellow shrugged. "No need."

For all he had to do was to lay one wee little finger aside his small nose and simply say, rather wearily, *"Facite! - Done!"*

For when he was still a tiny elf in short pants, Shorty Fay had attended a posh fairy Grammar School in a green hillside - and he liked to show off his classical learning whenever he could.

"What?"

"Already done."

"Oh …But remember, a fairy can never …"

But before Fergus could finish this reminder, a most powerful magical mist enveloped the famed Winnipeg Auditorium, a powerful mist of really potent fairy glamour. Colours became more muted and soft. More green. And the next moment …

Bejesus! And didn't Fergus suddenly find himself already fully kitted out and ready! -Suddenly out on the ice surface, standing at centre ice and ready for the puck drop and first face! – Bathed in a strange, shimmering emerald light, as if he had just been re-awakened -and, bejesus, there he was, indeed, suddenly at centre ice of the great, shimmering Winnipeg Auditorium, dramatically poised for the first drop. On his two feet, he could now feel the stiff leather of his new fairy ice-skates – and the wicked sharp blades beneath them. And in his two new cowhide mittens he felt a stout, wooden, enchanted fairy hockey stick!

The wee small little fellow had done it all! In the blink of an eye!

And there, too, poised opposite Fergus at centre ice, bending for the first face, was the famous, celebrated, god-like Dan Bain, exalted captain and centreman of the defending Stanley Cup Champion *Winnipeg Victorias!* - that great Winnipeg shinny god now actually stooping down for the dramatic first puck drop of the Cup challenge, as a Referee held out the rubber.

Fergus looked quickly around and found that the Barneyville Shamrocks, and all the other Victorias were at their position too, poised and ready!

"Gentlemen! *At the ready*!" ordered the referee, holding out the rubber to drop.

Thrilled, Fergus bent for the face, confidently feeling the old, glorious heft of a wooden hockey stick in his hands, the familiar edge of sharpened blades carving the ice under his feet, all tuned to fly.

The great Bain also hunched his shoulders and tensed for the face - but only after giving Fergus's new hockey gear an odd look.

It was only then, that Fergus O'Donnell himself, surprised by Bain's look, first thought to look down at his own new hockey stick.

"*Mother of God!*" Fergus suddenly howled in unmanned horror.

"What's the problem over there, Fergus?" called out Emmet Leary on the wing.

"*Bejesus! And will you look!* For he's only given me a *girly field hockey stick!*"

For, indeed, in his hands Fergus was embarrassingly holding a stubby school-girl's field hockey stick, not a proper ice-hockey weapon!

"*Horrors! And true on all of us!*" now cried out the other Shamrocks in dismay. For weren't they now *all* holding short little school-girly field hockey sticks, to the man of them! The Shamrocks had all embarrassingly been equipped entirely with girly field hockey sticks!

"These aren't proper, manly shinny sticks!"

"Mine's a foot too short!" cried Owen Smithers in surprise.

"And mine's got girly pink ribbons braided around the haft of it!" cried out Tommy Hankin in mortification. "And even girly love-knots tied onto the thing!"

"*Bejesus!* And how are we supposed to play with *these* feminine things?"

But it was too late! The fatal rubber had already been dropped! The game was already on!

Instantly, Dan Bain took the puck onto his own swift blade and swept it off to the wing.

Instinctively, the Shamrock Seven fanned out, leaping to the defence with their short little field hockey sticks.

But then:

"*Bejesus! - Look at us now!*"

For before any of the boys could take a second stride, they were all stumbling, tripping and sliding like bowling pins, in all directions across the ice.

"*Curses!*" shouted out Bartel Darcy, his face red with embarrassment. "*Look at this!* For I'm only wearing Ladies' Figure Skates!"

"Bad luck to us all! For we're *all* wearing ladies' figure skates!" shouted Tommy Hankin. "How did this happen? These things aren't manly shinny skates!"

"And they've only got girly *picks* on the front, as well!"

And so they did! The manly Shamrocks had all been magically outfitted in Ladies' Figure Skates! With nasty picks on the front! And all over the ice, Shamrocks were now digging in and tripping over their own toes, careening down to the ice, then trying to scramble up again, – but the unfamiliar, girly picks on the front of the blades kept catching the lads up – and again down they all went, falling and stumbling back onto the ice, like drunken sailors!

A loud howl of ridicule went up around the Winnipeg Auditorium.

"*Go, the Shamrock Girls!*"

"Gentlemen!" demanded the indignant referee. "Get up on your feet and play on! *Shameful!* You are making a spectacle of the Stanley Cup!""

"This is very bad on ourselves!" moaned Emmett Leary, crashing into the end boards.

"*Agreed!*" put in Owen Smithers, himself skidding and falling again flat on the ice. "And maybe it's surely we are indeed makin' the fools of ourselves!"

"And who's to blame for it now, I might ask you!"

"Well it's never myself!" called out young Tim Leary, who was watching in horror from the bench. "And don't be forever blaming the spare man!"

The fallen, tripping and sliding Shamrocks had now all gone red with shame and humiliation, as they skittered and spun in circles across the rink, crashing one by one off the boards, like out-of-control curling stones.

"Did ye no fetch along your curling brooms, laddies?" shouted another old crofter, taking the cue. "For no doubt ye've come to the wrong ice rink!"

The only Shamrock who was not skittering and sliding over the ice was Michael Davies, because he had fallen head-first into his own goal.

Finally, the humiliated Shamrocks managed to crab their way on hands and knees to the low boards, trying to catch onto some firm support.

"Oh dear, the wee little laddies are just learning to skatey-skate," crowed another witty spectator. "Fetch the poor, wee bairns some babby cheese-cutters!"

"Did yez come for the tobogganing, boys?" suggested another of the spectators.

And even the usually sporting *Victorias* were trying not to smile.

"Manners, chaps," ordered the gentlemanly Dan Bain, trying not to smile. "Give the ladies a hand."

"May I offer you my arm in assistance, my dear?" grinned one of the Flett brothers, bending down to assist Tommy Hankins.

"*And don't I wish I'd never come to Winny-peg!*"

For the mighty Shamrocks had never been so deeply humiliated in their young lives.

Poor Fergus himself finally had managed to crawl on his knees over to the penalty box, where the great famous silver cup itself was set out on a small table. But poor Fergus hardly glanced at it; instead he made a grab at the wee small fellow.

"Blast your soul, you dishonest little sprite*!*"

"Ah! And so it's now just myself, that you'll be blaming for all your own mistakes, is it?" protested the wee small fellow indignantly.

"I said *ice skates and hockey sticks*, and these are ... "

Fergus stopped cold. - *Oh no!* For technically, he was *indeed* wearing *ice* skates and holding a *hockey* stick.

"Yes, and bad manners to you!" protested the wee small fellow indignantly. "For what else should you be callin' those things?

"You knew what I meant! I meant *men's* ice-skates and sticks! These are for girlies!"

"Ah, but did you actually specify that, now?"

"*You knew …*"

"Hurley sticks or shillelaghs, certainly, that would have been clear to me, had you asked for those. - But, come to the matter fairly – what other persons in the western world would know the technicalities of your peculiar shinny game, when it's never been seen in any other civilized nation?"

"*That's not …*

"And with good reason for it, as I'm thinkin'. For all I've seen of your peculiar game is a lot of tripping and falling on your arses like fools - and how's that sorry spectacle ever to attract the punters, if you look to the financial side of it?"

"But you knew …!"

"- And more besides," stormed on the wee small little fellow, winding himself up now to full elfin indignation, "for at the end of all, what's even in it for the grand prize? But to be handed some old silver bowl from off the Governor General's dinner table and told to stuff it into your Gladstone bag and cart it along home on loan for a few days. - And a winning team can't even *keep* the thing, nor carry it down to the pawn for some cash."

"*May lightning strike you dead*!" gasped Emmett Leary, for he and the other boys had now crawled over on their hands and knees to join the conversation.

"Yes, this 'old silvery bowl' would be the Lord Stanley's *Cup*, you wee little heathen, not just some …"

"The Shamrocks have been humiliated and shamed entirely, Fergus O'Donnell!" cut in Owen Smithers accusingly.

"Too true, Owen Smithers," agreed all the others heatedly. "The deep disgrace is entirely bad on ourselves!"

"We'll now forever be the laughing-stock of all Puddle Township!"

"Every soul in Winnipeg, Manitoba is *already* mocking us!"

"This is all your fault, Fergus O'Donnell!"

"I wish I had never come!"

"*Agreed!*" cried an angry Tommy Hankin, getting right into Fergus's face. "*- For don't I myself wish that none of this had never, ever happened!*"

"*Ha!*" retorted Fergus with great heat, pushing at Tommy and finally losing his temper in frustration. "*And don't I entirely wish that one too, Tommy Hankin!*"

But then Fergus O'Donnell realized what his big mouth had rashly blurted.

"*No, wait!*"

But it was too late.

"Third wish then," ruled the wee small fellow.

"*No, wait! No, don't …* "

"*Never, ever happened.* – Done!"

"*No, wait!*"

But it was too late this time. And Fergus had not even had his fingers crossed.

"Never ever happened," repeated a wee, small, little voice, with satisfaction. "And feckin' glad of it I am, as well."

And that is why the hockey history books mistakenly say that no challenge was ever given to the Winnipeg Victorias, after the end-of-season in 1901.

***

All this story never happened a very long, long time ago. So today, if you should drive up to the vast lake country of Central

Ontario, and if on the way to the cottage you should visit the old lakeside hamlet of Barneyville (now called Rosedale-in-the Lakes), no matter how long you might comb through all the yellowing newspaper files of the town library, you will find no mention of the 1901 Barneyville Cup.

Nor, if you should go to the splendid city of Toronto and to the sacred Hockey Hall of Fame - nor even if you should study all the official hockey histories in all the archives of all the historical associations of the land – never, ever will you find it *not* stated, that in the year of 1901, no team ever came forward to challenge Winnipeg for their Stanley Cup - the *only* year in the entire early history of the challenge era, it is claimed, that the reigning champions were not called upon to defend their title. It was an event that never happened.

Officially because, as Mr. P.D. James reported in his splendid paper, *The Ottawa Evening Journal,* "Our noble Ottawa boys were just too darned banged up to challenge or to make the trip to Winnipeg this season-end."

("Cowardly custards," said Sheriff Sherwood.)

But now, you have learned the real truth. There was indeed a challenge for the Cup in 1901. It actually did happen. It is just that, later, it un-happened.

And, clearly, it was the match between Barneyville and the Winnipeg Victorias that hockey historians are always referring to, when they cite the cup challenge that never took place in 1901.

***

All this was a very long, long time ago. Today, a hundred and more years have passed. A long century has slowly slipped by.

But what is true, is that a hundred years ago, in all Puddle Township, up in the lake country of Central Ontario, it was indeed an Irish lad named Fergus O'Donnell who had the great name of the hockey player - starring at the centre ice position and leading the Barneyville Shamrocks to many the grand shinny victory and to many a glorious sporting trophy.

***

On one particular late autumn afternoon in the year 1921, not long after the Great War of 1914-18, another small boy of the town sat copying his detention lines in the new, four-roomed schoolhouse of Barneyville - but often idling with his pencil and gazing out at the choppy blue waters of Big Puddle Lake.

On that golden autumn afternoon, the old town wharf could still be seen, sagging out into the bay. But now, lying alongside the pier, appeared only the rusted funnel and the tilted wooden wheelhouse of the old *John A. Macdonald,* sticking up above the lapping waters of the shore; for it had been only two summers past that the faithful old lake steamer had finally sprung a leak and gone to the bottom. But near the town wharf, that afternoon, Jimmy Underhill's new Model T truck was nonetheless faithfully loading up freight and supplies at the CPR depot.

"Will you *please* be leaving off the daydreaming and be finishing your detention lines, young Charley O'Donnell" sighed Michael Davis, the middle-aged schoolmaster, pulling down his spectacles and peering from his own high desk into the empty classroom, at the boy. "Or you'll never get home to dinner. And then your mother, Mary O'Brien Farrell, and Fergus will be claiming my scalp, boyo."

"Yessir, Mr. Davies!"

I will never again dip Peggy Murray's pigtails in my ink-well, Charley O'Donnell wrote on one side of his lined foolscap paper; and then on the other side: "*The capital of the Province of*

Saskatchewan is Regina. Many new immigrants have gone there. The capital of Alberta is ... Vancouver. And the capital of ... "

"Sir! Sir!"

"Be-jeepers, Charley! Will you just be hunting out the correct matter from the school geography for yourself and stop interrupting me at my own work!" sighed Michael Davies, setting down his pen from the compositions he was marking.

"No, no, sir! Another question, sir!"

"Oh, dear, and what would that be this time?"

"Sir, you played hockey when you were young, didn't you?"

"I did that – I did. But don't try any more of your tricks to come 'round me and get out of doing your lines and lessons."

"But, sir, sir! What position did you play at?"

"I was the goaltender," said Michael.

"You played with my dad, didn't you? On the old Shamrocks?"

"I did so. I played with Fergus and Tommy Hankin and the other boys when we were all young fellas in the village."

"My dad was a good player, wasn't he?"

"Oh, yes indeed. In all Puddle Township, Fergus was the boy."

"And the Shamrocks won a lot of trophies, didn't they?"

"I suppose we did. - Champions of Puddle, 1896-1901. And three times more of it, later."

"*Wow!* And did you ever win the *Porcupine?*"

"*Ah!* We never did that, worse luck. Just missed it, in 1906 and again in 1911 – but then the younger boys, like Tim Leary and Johnny Pincombe, went off to the War. - That was pretty much the end of the old Shamrocks."

"Did the Shamrocks ever win the Stanley Cup?"

"*Goodness, no!*" chuckled Michael Davies. "What an idea! That was too grand for the likes of us! No, no, that never happened. We were just the backwoods colonial boys."

"Sir?"

"What now?"

"Did my dad's cousin play on the Shamrocks too?"

"If it's that wee little sneaky fellow, Shorty Fay, that you'd be speaking of? No, no."

"Where did he go?"

"Well, nobody knows. One day, he just sloped off and departed. It's a mystery."

"Olden days history is sort of interesting to learn about, isn't it, Mr. Davies?"

"More interesting than writing your detention lines, would that be?"

Charley blushed and for a few minutes copied a few more lines.

"When I grow up, I'm going to be a detective and solve mysteries like that."

"Well, perhaps you could. Plenty of mysteries to solve there, Charley. But first, you'd better to solve some Geography. Let's see your lines."

"Oh dear!" frowned Michael. "Look here. You've still only got eight of our nine Provinces, boy. What's the missing one?"

"Ah ... might it be *California*?"

"No, no."

"*Alaska*?"

"It might be that. But look it up for yourself in the geography, boy. Don't be asking your teacher to be giving you all the answers."

In a few moments, Charley O'Donnell shouted out eagerly: "Oh yeah, I've got it now, sir!"

"Yes?"

"It's *Manitoba*!"

Michael Davies looked up with a start. Then, a strange, misty, greenish vapour of ghostly memory seemed to seep into the old Barneyville schoolhouse, and Michael Davies eyes misted over and took on a faint, faraway expression.

"And the capital of the Province of Manitoba is *Winnipeg*! - Am I right now? - Sir? Sir?"

But Michael Davies was no longer listening. For just now, once again that strangely elfin glamour seemed to seep and steal mystically over the Barneyville schoolroom, a kind of spell of misty enchantment and fairy magic. And for Michael Davies, everything now began to be more softly defined, more dream-like, more magical. Sounds were more hushed and colours more vibrant. More green.

And then, strangely, Michael found himself feeling a lonely, unaccountable emptiness and an old, sad, ghostly yearning, for slapping pucks and cutting blades.

"Sir! I'm finished!"

But for a long dreamy moment, Michael Davies did not reply. A strange half-memory still seemed to filter through the schoolroom. And an even stranger tickling seemed to run over his tongue – a sort of emerald, Hibernian tickling, a feeling which he had long forgotten over the many, many years since he and Fergus, and Tommy Hankin, and Rory Burn, and Emmet Leary and all the other boys had been young, strapping, émigré lads on the shores of the Big Puddle, learning and playing the grand Canadian game of shinny, down by the frozen marshes, beside the famous, frozen Barneyville town pond.

"I think I'll be a famous history guy when *I* grow up, not a detective," said Charley. "Because all the funny old things that happened in history are really interesting to find out about, aren't they, sir?"

"They are that, indeed," agreed Michael Davies. "Things that happened in history are always interesting."

- But what Michael Davies, the schoolmaster, was actually thinking, as the last wisps of that strange greenish enchantment lingered in the schoolroom … was that the most interesting stories in history are really the ones that *never* actually happened.

****

THE STORY OF LEYLAND DUMFRIES, "THE CRICK POET"

"Children," said Mr. Allen Crouch, the rural schoolmaster, adjusting his wire-framed eye-glass, "on this, our very last afternoon of school before your summer vacation, the provincial Education Department wants all elementary school pupils to hear an important *notification*, regarding next year's Grade 6 Literature Project. Ahem …"

"*Sir! Sir! Teacher!* - What's '*nortification*', like what you just said?"

"Barbara," sighed Mr. Crouch, frowning at a small girl in the second row of desks, "just *listen? - Then* questions?"

"I were only just askin'!"

"Don't cry, Barbara."

Mr. Crouch re-adjusted his pince-nez, straightened his celluloid collar, then carefully continued: "Children, as our school year of 1887-1888 comes to its highly gratifying ending, the Department in Toronto wants all small elementary children to reflect upon our great National … National … *something* … *Ah!* Our great National *Progress and Advancement* … Sea -to-Shining-Sea. As it were. - Thus, over the vacation, the Department wants each of you to reflect upon new ways in which we may all further our destined National Advance … Advancement."

"Children, our strong, newly emerging, northerly Dominion – the great infant Dominion of Canada - has now … *is* now a … a miniscule new …. *Sorry!* That's '*muscular*' new nation … proud new Giant of the North … Eldest Son of … of our glorious Brit … British Mother … *Britannia!*"

"*Hip, hip …!*"

"Thank you, Barbara. … But … but our new young Dominion will not … *cannot* … achieve its full destiny of greatness … until it has found and expressed its own unique … identity … and … and given voice to its own unique stories and poetry – odes, elegies, a few Petrarchan Sonnets, that sort of thing."

"*Sir! Sir! Mister!* D' you b'lieve what that there book says?"

"I am a professional *educator*, Barbara," sighed Mr. Crouch. "I personally don't have to believe anything. I just have to read you what the Education Department instructs me to read, in the Curriculum."

"*Sir! Sir! My favver* says we just need more iron-works."

"Well, your father is *wrong*, Barbara. Be quiet or see me for detention after school."

Mr. Allen Crouch frowned and tried again to find his place in his Department of Education Circular. Finally, he put his finger upon the passage about *Objectives for the Literary Arts for 1888-1889,* then he went on:

"… Thus, a truly *true* national identity can never be authentically achieved, until our rising new Dominion has seized and won its own place upon the sacred elevations of Mount… Mount *Parnassus* … by also creating its own … its own unique, inspired, national *Narrative Epic,* in verse, 24 books, in High elevated classical dictation – no- sorry -*Diction*, - as well as in a sublime, noble form of versification, such as: *"Hark! Hark! / The dogs do bark! / The beggars are coming to town!"*

"Sir! Sir! *Please*, sir!"

"Oh dear… But very well, Barbara," sighed Mr. Crouch. "What's the question this time?"

"What's this 'ere, *Parnacalus* you was goin' on about?

Mr. Crouch frowned awkwardly. But fortunately, there was assistance at hand, in a footnote.

"*Parnassus* ... children ... *Mount* Parnassus was, as is well-known, a famous mountainside in the ancient times, long before today, where a great deal of old poetry stuff was once copied down. - On clay, or perhaps wax tablets, I should think," explained Mr. Crouch, examining the footnote at the bottom of the circular.

"But why did they have to write it on a *mountain*, sir?" piped up another squeaky voice.

"It was *High* Classical Poetry, Leyland, which was 'elevated' in 'subject, tone and language'. So they had to get up onto a high place to do it."

Not long after this, young Mr. Crouch shut up his teaching shop for the year. The very last school day had blessedly arrived. Summer Holidays began.

"Remember, children! During this coming summer, I want each of you to reflect upon the challenge you have just heard," ordered Mr. Crouch, as the children rushed out the schoolhouse door, across the grassy schoolyard, and then off through the pine grove which encircled their rural place of higher learning.

"- *Ere! What a load of old cod's wallop!*" said little Barbara Bantry to her friend Leyland Dumfries, as they both trotted away home, hand-in-hand, through the Pinery, then through two corn fields and a cow pasture, towards the rural hamlet of Gormley Centre. "Never 'eard nuffink so daft, 'ave I? *Parnassus!* - It's flat as a bleedin' pancake 'round 'ere!"

Leyland was always rather intimidated by the direct-talking Barbara, as he was only a rural Ontario boy, and she a recent, sophisticated émigré from the inner streets of London England itself! Where Queen Victoria lived!

"Have you ever seen the Queen yourself, Barbara?" Leyland once asked.

"Course I 'ave," said Barbara. "We lived just 'round the corner from 'er, didn't we? In Pimlico."

After that, Leyland never dared to contradict Barbara again.

But as he and Barbara trotted home from the schoolhouse that June afternoon, with their lunch pails and calico book satchels, Leyland was pretty excited by what Mr. Crouch had just told them - all about poetical-type verse stuff and Parnacalus! *To write the great Canadian Epic*! In verse! *And to be the first*! - Leyland's emerging poetical soul was mightily awakened!

But there was no time to waste, Mr. Crouch had cautioned. The other British colonies and coming New Dominions would also be hard upon the same, great, competitive quest – Australia, New Zealand, and those other red-coloured-places on the map, which also proudly flew the Union Jack.

For apparently, as Leyland now understood the matter, in the year of 1888 there was a kind of Imperialist Arms-Race, to see which of the new, young British heirs and embryo nations would become top infant literary dog. - But, surely, said Mr. Crouch, that Place of Honour must rightfully go to Canada, first Dominion in the whole British Empire. Canada must reach the summit of Parnassus *first*!

"*- Go it, the Canadians*!"

"Thank you, Barbara. Again."

- But Mr. Crouch had also cautioned that each newly fledged British territory must first *discover* its own unique *National Essence - Its Own National Soul and Being-ness* - in order to pull off the job. No National Essence nor Being-ness, no Parnassus.

Mr. Crouch had then paused for effect.

"- So, Children, what could *be*, what *is*, the essence unique to our very own Noble Northern Dominion? Look about you, children. Compare. What essence, for example, does our great sister, Australia, have that is unique to *her* national territory and soul? Or New Zealand? Or …

"Kangaroos!" someone shouted enthusiastically.

"Wallabees!" someone else suggested.

"Boomerangs!" cried out a third.

"Zealands!"

"Grand start, Children!" exclaimed Mr. Crouch, enthusiastically. "*Find the essence of our burgeoning nation's soul!* Already, our Australian and New Zealand cousins, our noble sister territories in our great Imperial British Empire, are hard, hard at work, creating Kangaroo Odes, Wallabee Verses, and Boomerang Lyrics! Our own rising young poets must work harder, to catch up! - So … what do *we*, here in Canada, uniquely possess, exemplifying our own unique national *soul?*

"Beavers!" chimed in several of the pupils.

"Two-dollar bills!" offered some others.

"Eatons Department Store!"

True, said Mr. Crouch. But our American friends to the south also have beavers. And there was once a European beaver.

"Eatons Department Store!" shouted the others, doubling-down.

"Certainly, a good start," said Mr. Crouch. "But over the summer, the Department of Education wants each of you to search your growing minds, for some symbol, some essential *essence*, unique to our own Dominion. Answers to be handed in, after Labour Day."

"Eatons Department Store!"

"That was already suggested, Leyland. Use the summer holiday to reflect and think of something new and more original, please."

Leyland was very excited. For the truth was, Leyland had always had a puzzling inner feeling about himself, which this new challenge now deeply stirred.

"An't you stoppin' at our place, Leyland?" said Barbara. "You're invited. Mum's got bread and jam."

"Well …"

"And milk. We got our own cow now."

"Well … tell your mother I can't come over today, sorry," Leyland apologized. "I have to do chores for Uncle Jack."

"I've got a new rabbit and all. You could see her."

"Can't today, Barbara. Sorry. Tell your mum."

"You're just *mean*!"

"Don't cry, Barbara. Maybe tomorrow."

For the truth was, Leyland was eager to rush home to his uncle's farmhouse, at the other edge of Gormley Centre, to dig out his old scribbler and pencils, and to get going on his own important Poetical Epic. With 24 Books to scribble before September, time was pressing.

For, full of new hope, Leyland Dumfries believed that he had just been awakened to a new, powerful calling, which he did not yet quite understand. But Nature endows its divine gifts more lavishly on some rural schoolhouse pupils, than others. Some pupils are called to be Engineers, Architects, Farmers, or Eatons Department Store Salespersons. But some – the rare few- are called to be Poets. And from his earliest boyhood, Leyland had felt a confusing, versifying sort of broodiness, whenever he went roaming and moping through a bosky grove or a scrub bush swamp - or when he sat idly lolling and dreaming in the shades of the willow trees, down by Bungman's Crick, that muddy little stream. But never until today had Leyland felt the call so viscerally.

"Well, she's probably just wind and indigestion, boy," said his Uncle Jack, that night at supper in the farmhouse kitchen, when Leyland excitedly related what Mr. Allen Crouch has told them. "Take a spoonful of the Potion, boy, she's in the outhouse," advised Uncle Jack, making a hand-rolled cigarette and striking a sulphur match on the worn knee of his overalls.

- For, alas, even in those later settlement days, when only pockets of bush remained to be cleared, Canada had not yet become the sensitive, cultured, poetical-type nation that it is today.

Even as late as 1888, few of the now-elderly pioneer folk, nor their younger offspring, the current rural farmers, had personally felt the high poetical call of Nature.

"Nothin' sublime about this damned country, boy," his Uncle Jack often grumbled, "as it's been nothing to date but just clearin' bush and choppin' down more damned, bloody trees."

Thus, the only contribution Uncle jack ever made to Canadian *Literchur* came one solitary winter evening, while Leyland was trying to compose a sensitive verse, and Jack sat hunched by the McClary kitchen range, honing his double-bladed bush axe. That contribution was a curt, sardonic couplet, scribbled into the margin of Leyland's *A Harvest Basket of Golden Verse for Ontario Schools, Grades V-VI*.

I hope that I shall never see
A sight so sickening as another bloody tree.

This unpoetical attitude, Leyland later recalled, was typical of our early, horny-handed bush-whackers. For, in those earlier days, the culture of our new Dominion was almost entirely ruled by *Utter Insensitive Philistines* – as Leyland fondly recollected in his later memoir, *To Pluck A Rural Reed*. (*A Rural Weed*, his Uncle Jack called it.)

"Ninety-nine percent of poems today are pretty much mostly crap," said Uncle Jack. "But you're a moony lad, Leyland, so give it a go. - *After* chores."

But where to begin? All that summer, no inspiration came to Leyland, no divine call, no essence. And so, it was with some dejection that Leyland Dumfries returned to the old four-roomed schoolhouse that next September, still with nothing original in his imagination, in the way of a truly Canadian *essence*.

Other pupils had been more industrious.

"Now children," said Mr. Crouch. "The Department and perhaps myself have been eager to hear what poetical-type imaginative nourishment, what truly, distinctively Canadian versificantory soul-food and *essences* have we all thought of, over our summer holiday? Truly Canadian, mind you!

"Butter tarts!"

"Butter tarts – but ordered from Eatons Department Store!" challenged others, raising the bar.

"Blended Rye Whiskey! Yum, Yum!"

"Go stand in the corner, Leonard Pyle," said Mr. Crouch. "And be kind enough to visit me after school."

"But alas, children, it is not nourishment for the *mortal belly* which we are seeking – but nourishment for the poetical-type soul! We must all strive further!"

To give them more help, Mr. Allen Crouch now confided another important rule. All poetical-type inspirations are received from one single source alone, he now revealed to them - and that source was the sublime grandeur of *Unspoiled Natural Beauty!* This poetical fact and new discovery had been absolutely proven by some old type named J. Keats, Mr. Crouch said, reading from his book.

"Oi! I know 'im*!*" whispered Barbara, suddenly paying more attention. "That's old Jacky Keats! 'E 'ad a barrow, just down our street in Lambeff! -But *'e* weren't no poet!"

But the fact that Mr. Crouch had made this connection impressed Barbara enough, that henceforth she always showed more respect for poetry. But then Barbara was always more interested in school subjects that she already knew about.

One day, during a lesson on the many excellent military and naval victories of Our Empire, Barbara looked at a drawing Leyland was making, inside the cover of his Department of Education history primer, *Loyal Tales of Our Heroic British Past.* 2nd Edition.

Barbara bent closer. "Oo's that old git?" she asked. "What you're drawin'?"

"It's Lord Nelson, who won the famous Battle of Terfalgar!"

"Oh, I know 'im too! 'E 'ad a Pub, over the road from us. In Bermondsey."

But as that autumn of 1888 wore on, and as the maple, chestnut and elm leaves began to redden and to fall - and despite Mr. Crouch's expert mentoring - Leyland still had not found any true poetical essence, to stuff into verse. Much as he moped among the cows grazing in the autumn meadows or idled through the wilting corn fields on his way home with Barbara to Gormley Centre, no divine inspiration from Unspoiled Natural Beauty seemed truly to inspire him, in a full and proper swooning fashion, such as J. Keats recommended.

But Leyland could not let his hopes go. For Mr. Allen Crouch had inadvertently planted a dangerous idea in young Leyland's mind, a belief and a desire about himself, that would mislead and bother Leyland for years.

- But then Leyland recalled another thing that Mr. Crouch had said earlier that September — or had read - from the Ontario Educational Department Curriculum! Something which Leyland had not paid sufficient attention to at the time! But which, now, suddenly, came back to him!

"Children," had said Mr. Crouch, running his inky forefinger across a further sentence in the Curriculum, "not only must a true inspiration of poetry come from an elevated place and from unspoiled natural beauty, it must always … *flow*. It must be a *free and flowing* inspiration of the … the, …wait a moment, … ah! … *of the free and flowing inspirational power* of some natural graceful object … Copy that down, please."

At the time, Leyland had failed to copy down that important, poetical-type, insider information into his Scribbler — as, at the moment, Barbara Bantry was showing him a comic postcard, from her last family holiday excursion to the seaside.

"Look 'ere!" she whispered. "They got a great long Pier, and donkeys, and a Punch and Judy and …"

"Did you see *all that*?" Leyland whispered in awe.

"Course I did."

But the subliminal retention of any true, poetical-type Imagination is amazing. For now, weeks later, in deepest autumn, Mr. Crouch's words magically returned and resurfaced from Leyland's unconscious mind!

"Flowing and Streaming!"

In a flash, Leyland flung down his hoe (he was bedding up a turnip and onion patch for winter) and excitedly raced to the ramshackle summer kitchen, where Leyland urgently rooted among the galvanized milk pails and manure forks for his rubber boots and poetry notebook!

"Flowing and Streaming!"

Leyland now understood *exactly* where he must go to find poetical inspiration! Across the farm yard, past the hog pen, around the unpainted barn Leyland scrambled. Then, flinging open a leaning field gate, onward he ran, across a meadow of grazing cows, through a parching corn field of the back forty, and then on over the last rail fence – until he had reached the creek- flats of old Bungman's Crick, winding and lazily flowing along under the drooping willow trees!

Bungman's Crick! But why had Leyland never before seized the natural and powerful poetical potential of good old, slow-meandering Bungman's Crick? *Flowing! - and right under his nose!* But why had it taken him so long to get it? - J. Keats would have scoped out the versifical-type potentials of Bungman's Crick and banged out 16 lines for immortality, straight off, first time up at the wickets!

A Crick of Beauty is a joy forever.
It will hardly never ever ...

But could he, 12-year-old Leyand Dumfries, or any other rustic, rough-hewn, culturally-deprived colonial boy in raw, rural Canada, ever, *ever*, match such elegant British-born genius as that of those real native-born Scotch and English guys who got printed up in the school anthology, like W. Shakespeare, *Gent.* Or Wilfred Tennyson, whose rousing "Charge of the Late Brigade" Leyland adored so much.

("Oi! - I know 'im too!" little Barbara had said.)

But soon Leyland was down beside the little stream, deep under the willow shadow and the over-arching glade of Bungman's Crick itself! – What Natural Rural Beauty! - and in that magical flickering of light and shade, Leyland flung himself down on the grassy bank of the creek and pulled out his pencil and scribbler, intently watching the old brown, slow-moving stream – waiting for inspiration!

How lovely it all was! All through his rural boyhood, Leyland Dumfries had passed many dreamy hours of springtime, summer, and golden autumn, down beside this beloved little stream, bob-fishing for small perch, winging chestnuts with his sling-shot at basking snapping turtles, or just watching black squirrels and sparrows and other foresty-type creatures, skipping and frisking from branch to branch overhead, frolicking merrily in the golden sunlight, the little birds twittering and singing, and the black squirrels bashing up one another, higher up in the gnarled willow trees.

Then, in a truly magical moment, Leyland caught a sudden glimpse of brilliant, flashing colour - a swift-darting kingfisher, flashing like a bright arrow under the low-trailing curtain and veils of the leaning willows, sweeping low along the current of the stream, cutting unerringly under the low-drooping shadows of the gnarled trees, as if to kiss and caress the brown waters of Bungman's Crick – and now …

- Then with a shock - and with a leap of excitement! - Leyland suddenly realized that what he had just said, *right inside himself,* might almost be Poetry! The simple, humble poetry of the natural, rural world of his own enlivened boyhood and youth!

ODE TO A KINGFISHER
By Leyland Dumfries, aged 12

*

Hail to thee, bright spirit!
Bored thou never weren't

So generally active and energetic by Bungman's Crick,
Where oft-times many willows lean like leaning streamside trees!
Amid the buzzing of some bees!

It was only five lines and vaguely derivative, and the rhyme scheme might need some polishing, but it was Leyland's very own, first real poem!

Leyland ran straight to Barbara's house, to show her.

"*Cor! Lovely!*" said Barbara. "That last one about the bees is grand!"

"You like it, then? You figure I could be a poet?"

"Course I do," said Barbara.

This encouragement was wonderfully reinforcing to Leyland. Now he felt really, really hopeful that he was on a good track, in the poetical line of work.

Next day in the schoolyard, at recess, he showed his poem to his rival, Leonard Pyle.

"Total crap," said Leonard. "Nobody writes that old kind of nature-moony-sentimental twaddle nowadays. *Kingfishers and little huzzy-buzzy humble bees*! Get aboard the future, Dumfries. Symbolism is the real ticket now."

"What's that?" asked Leyland.

"Oh, *puh-lease*!" sighed Leonard. "How *Provincial*."

"How *wearisome*," Leonard added, with a fatigued sigh.

"'Ere!" said Barbara fiercely. "Don't pay no mind to 'im! Snooty git!"

And Barbara picked up stones and started pelting Leonard Pyle, until he ran away.

"*Ow! Ow! Stoppit!*" howled Leonard Pyle.

"*Clear off!*" Barbara was little, but she had a wicked throwing arm – and later became the excellent fastball pitcher for the Gormley Centre girls' provincial championship team.

But chill winter was approaching, and still Leyland had not hit on another further solid essence, not even one drop for even another single line of uniquely Canadian Verse

"Just keep scribblin', in't it?" recommended Barbara. "'*Scribble, scribble, scribble, eh, Mr. Gibbon?*' Like wot old King George said to old Gibby at the palace."

"Wherever did you learn *that*!!" exclaimed Leyland in astonishment.

"Back 'ome, weren't I? When we was doin' that old tosh about-whatsit? Decline and … somefink, somefink, weren't it?"

"Little school children study *that* in England?"

"Course we do."

"You *read* that?"

"Course I did."

Now Leyland felt even more shamefully provincial.

"Old Augy Caesar- and all that dead lot - emperor this, emperor that," Barbara now remembered. "*Cor!*"

"You *learned* all that?"

"Course I did, didn't I? - We 'ad to, didn't we? Else you got the slipper."

Now Leyland felt incredibly *even more ignorant and provincial.* Real British children back in the mother country were so much more advanced than out-sourced British-Canadian children over here! But Mr. Allen Crouch and the Department of Education had aroused a glimmering, phosphorescent, and alluring ambition in Leyland. So Leyland plodded on, hopefully.

The frosts of November came. Then arrived the snow and the freezing weather of December. Over Christmas, the land was frost-bound and hard. But then in the early New Year came a brief melt and two days of heavy rain, before the temperature dropped again, leaving a glittering, icy sheen on the fields and barnyard. Next day, the sun returned, but the world remained iron and chilled.

That morning, Leyland rose early; and, after chores, he hiked out into the frozen meadows and fields, crunching through the frosty surface in his rubber boots, fascinated by the gleaming glitter and reflections of the morning sun on the icy landscape.

Leyland eventually wandered up onto a high field crest, looking down into the still and silent flats of Bungman's Creek. The trees along the crick were bare now, and Leyland could see the gleaming, frozen stream winding and curving away for miles; for after the rains, the surface of the crick was transformed into a perfectly smooth, shining mirror! Brilliantly glazed for miles, without a patch of snow or break anywhere! Magic! Leyland stood fascinated, awed by such a natural, perfect skating surface, that comes only a few times in a lifetime!

But then, suddenly, there was a flash of colour, a bright arrow flashing down the surface of the mirror-like crick!

But not a bright kingfisher this time. It was a girl! A girl in a thick, white, woollen Arran sweater and a long skirt – a girl with a bright red toque on her head and a red scarf streaming behind. An elegant, slender girl on speed-skates, flashing and blading it down the glittering surface of Bungman's Crick in the bright-morning sunshine! *Going like a rocket!*

Leyland was stunned. Who was she? Where was she going?

It was a vision of grace and extraordinary skill! What elegant stride! What finesse! What brilliant skating! What a magical girl!

For a moment, the slender, racing girl disappeared behind a small bend in the crick, then Leyland caught another flash of her, further down the creek, burning along. Who was she?

Leyland had to find out. He went down the slope, slipping and sliding onto the frozen crick; then, scrambling as hard as he could, he followed after the mysterious girl! It was dangerous going up the smooth crick, Leyland's slippery rubber boots threatening to spill him any moment. But he persevered. It must have been a quarter-mile or so, before Leyland turned a narrow bend and came upon an amazing scene.

There again was the girl in the red toque and scarf, but not alone now. Five other girls on skates, warmly clad in heavy knitted sweaters, scarves, and warm, plaid skirts, were gathered with her. And they all had hockey sticks and pucks!

Amazon girls, playing shinny!

"Hey, Dumfries!" shouted out one of the gang, spotting Leyland. *"Take off, eh? Girls only!"*

The tough shinny-playing girls now fiercely surrounded poor Leyland.

"Yeah! Take a hike, eh, Leyland! No boys!!"

"Yeah. Because we were here first, eh?"

Leyland now recognized the six. They were the big girls from school., Grade 8. Leyland was already a bit afraid of that mob. They were pretty tough. They could pull your hair or pinch you pretty badly, if you crossed them.

"Pack off, squirt!" ordered one girl named Gilly Fenton, menacing with her hockey stick. "This is our secret place, eh?"

"You can't be in the club," repeated Jeannie Clarke. "No boys."

But then the graceful, slender girl intervened. "Aw, that's only *Leyland*," she said. "Leave him alone."

"No, c'mon, let's roast the little twirp, Aylie," suggested Amy Dutton. Then she added: "You're in real big trouble now, Leyland. Nobody is supposed to know about the Secret Six. It's a secret."

"*A-my!*" protested all the girls shrilly. "*You're not supposed to give away our secret name, you moron!*"

"*Curses!* I forgot."

"You moron."

"Now you've spoiled the whole secret club, you dimwit."

"Well, then just roast him," argued Amy, with a pout. "So he can't tell."

But now the tall, slim girl intervened again. "No, leave him alone," she ordered. "He's just Leyland."

"Aileen!"

And now Leyland realized that the slim, graceful girl he had admired flashing along the creek was none other than the great and daring *Aileen Baird!* - The most graceful, the most admired, the most heroic girl in all Gormley Centre!

All the boys in P.S. 34, Gormley Centre, were madly in puppy-love with Aileen Baird!

Her father, Duff Baird, was one of the most prosperous farmers in the county, chair of the local Agricultural Board, Chairman of the School Council, and President of the Conservative Party in the local Riding.

And his daughter was supreme, top rung, most awesome girl-leader in all Gormley Centre. At school, all the smaller boys watched Aileen Baird with infatuation. Most of them said they were going to marry her, when they grew taller than four-foot-eight. But Aileen's social circle of sophisticated Grade 8 girls never mixed with younger persons in the schoolyard, being too mature and worldly for twirpy, junior boys like Leyland and his pals.

Leyland was pretty nervous now. The Secret Six were very powerful girls. They had once ganged up on Arthur Fraser in the schoolyard and pulled down his knickerbockers, embarrassingly revealing his Stanfield"s winter long johns. Leyland was terrified that they might be about to do the same to him.

"Leave Leyland alone," repeated Aylie Baird.

"Yeah, but he's spoiling the game!" protested Lorna Thompson. "And he knows our secret place."

"Naw, we'll let him stay," decided Aileen Baird. "He can play goal."

"*Aylie!* Girls only."

"He's cute."

"*Aylie!!*"

"*Aylie's got a crush! Aylie's got a crush!*"

"Stuff it, Fenton," said Aileen Baird, showing a fisted mitten.

"Wait 'till Tommy Faulds hears!" said Annie McTavish. "You're *dead*, Leyland!"

Now Leyland was really terrified. Tommy Faulds was the toughest boy in school. Tom Faulds had made it publicly known that he would murder any kid who came near Aileen Baird, his girlfriend. Aileen, of course, said Tom Faulds wasn't her boyfriend, the bucket-head. But Tom Faulds said he was – and he'd massacre anybody who wanted to challenge him. Leyland Dumfries certainly didn't want to get into the middle of *that!*

"So - go play goal then, Dumfries," grumbled Gilly Fenton. "Watch your nuts."

All the girls giggled. Leyland blushed to the roots, entirely shocked. *Girls talked like that? When their mothers weren't around?* Leyland could not believe it.

On the other hand, most of the small lads of Gormley Centre swore like troopers themselves - when *their* mothers weren't around. So Leyland decided it was alright -and quickly did what he was told.

Leyland was on Aileen Baird's team. His goal posts were a pair of rubber boots.

"Just stand there, Leyland," ordered Aileen Baird, "but don't let any pucks get in. Or else."

"Yeah, no blubbering, or jumping out the way on the hard ones, Dumfries," added Gilly Fenton. "Die at your post like a man. Or we'll kill you."

The opposite goal was marked by two rocks.

"Hey!" Annie McTavish protested. "Your crummy lot got a goalie! We haven't! No fair!"

"Yes, it is. - First dibs! We called first!"

"No, you didn't! You didn't even call choose ups!"

"We did!"

"You did not, Jeannie Clarke!"

"*Girls!*" Aileen said. "It's not a real goalie, it's only Leyland. Let's go. Who's got a puck?"

In the end the dispute was settled by putting a third rock in the centre of the other goal mouth, to represent another goaltender.

"No lifters or slappers at that end!" ruled Aileen Baird.

"What about Leyland?"

"Fire away," decided Aileen, shaking loose her brilliant red hair.

That was the very first time that Leyland Dumfries had ever played ice-hockey! He did not even know how to skate yet. He did not even own a pair of skates.

("What a *dink*!" said Leonard Pyle.)

But fortunately, in traditional crick hockey, goalies can play nets in rubber boots, and even without a stick. So that first day, Leyland Dumfries did so, standing up like a shaky fence-post, blocking shots - and only occasionally running away.

"Don't be so craven *yellow*, Leyland! It wasn't *that* hard!"

The game went on fiercely most of the afternoon, the Secret Six whizzing and passing and body-checking up and down the ice, until the late winter afternoon light was fading. When time was finally called, Leyland was so bruised and sore from pucks to the shins, that he could hardly stagger to the bank of the crick. For these demure, plaid-skirted, shinny-playing girls could all fire hard lifters and wristers - and also hammer home the slappers – although there weren't many slap-shots, as most of those skipped off and tunneled into a snow bank, where it took hours to dig them out again.

"No more slappers!" decreed Aileen Baird, as darkness was coming on. "Last puck!"

In fact, the game ended, as usual, only when a pale wintry moon had appeared through the bare tree tops- and when that very last puck was also lost - shot through Leyland's shaking legs and skittering down the crick about 40 yards, then straight into an otter family's doorway, where it could never be retrieved. The Secret Six still tried to play on, though, with a small flat rock, rather than give up the game, as all proper shinny players will do; but that wasn't as much fun. And Leyland was very gratified when time finally *was* called, as rocks are especially not-much-fun, if you are the goalie. Also, his fingers and toes were frozen – and slapshots to frozen toes in thin rubber boots are particularly unpleasant.

But all in all, Leyland felt he had done pretty well.

"Crikes, no way!!" groaned Gilly Fenton. "You were completely pathetic. Where did you learn to play goal?"

"But I never did. I never played hockey before."

"Don't ever try again," advised Amy Dutton. "You're useless. Girls play better, anyways."

"Yeah, that's for sure! 'Cause hockey is really a girls' sport."

"Go home now, Leyland," said Aileen Baird, softly, "but thanks for coming out."

"*Aylie's got a boyfriend!*"

"Shut it, Fenton."

"But know this, Dumfries," warned Jeannie Clarke in a sinister voice, "if you ever tell anybody about our secret place, we'll murder and kill you dead."

"Yeah. Be warned, Dumfries! *The Skull* is watching you!"

"Yeah! Even in your room at night! When you think you are all alone! All-alone-in-your-dark-dark-room! With nobody to hear you scream! - *Mommy!*"

"*Beware the Skull!*"

Well, if Leyland had been frightened by these daring and dangerous girls before, now he was absolutely terrified.

"Tell anybody, and we'll get you, Leyland!" Annie McTavish called out, as Leyland quickly scampered off into the growing dark, towards the dim, yellow, lantern-light of the home farm.

Nonetheless, at supper that night, Leyland did tell Uncle Jack.

"You played crick hockey for the first time in your life - with *girls*?" Uncle Jack said in astonishment. "*Jeez!* Don't tell anybody!"

"*Scary* girls," murmured Leyland.

"Still not right!" protested Jack, now deeply worried about his *protégé*. – First, poetry, now this. This boy needed to find a practical, down-to-earth focus to his life.

For now Uncle Jack was convinced, that Leyland had been kept in school far too long. Grade IV was about all any sensible rural boy needed these days, Jack grumbled, without airy-faery teachers putting radical, advanced, namby-pamby ideas and ambitions into his head. - Girls, sure. But not boys.

But all that night, in bed in his attic room, Leyland dreamt of *glorious crick hockey*! *What a game*! The thrill and bliss of frosty winter air! *And daring girls*! - And on his beloved crick, as well! For

Leyland had never before suspected the glorious winter happiness of a frozen crick, flashing blades and pucks! *And daring girls!* Why had nobody told him!

All that week in the schoolroom, Leyland drew wishful pictures of stick-men playing shinny! With admiring stick-girls watching!

"Wot's that, then?" asked Barbara, leaning over to look. "They got no bodies, just 'eads."

"It's symbolism."

"*That's* not symbolism!" scorned Leonard Pyle. "That's just crappy draughtsmanship."

Leyland now day-dreamed a lot about heroic, daring girls, of course. And, hopefully, being again invited to play shinny. At recess, Leyland trotted around the schoolyard, trailing after Aileen and her comrades like a hopeful puppy

"*Hey!* Just take off, *will you*, Leyland?" finally exclaimed Gillian Fenton in exasperation. "Just because you got to play goalie once, doesn't mean you can be in our club. Stop following us around!"

"Yeah, Dumfries! Take a hike, eh?"

"He's trying to eavesdrop on all our secret, private plans and stuff, Aileen!"

Leyland blushed and thereafter kept his distance – especially when he noticed Tommy Faulds giving him the evil eye.

"What *ho*, eh, Dumfries?" gloated Leonard Pyle, who had also been carefully watching. "Eh? Eh?"

"I wasn't doin' anything! Leave me alone."

But it seemed to Leyland that his poetical-type imagination was now deeply, creatively *galvanized*! That night at the kitchen table, a miraculous thing happened! Leyland had hardly planted both elbows on the worn oilcloth and bent to composition, when lines of clumsy *shinny verse* started pouring out, into his old school scribbler! It just happened! Magically!

Uncle Jack was puzzled.

"How the *devil* did you get from stalkin' some older woman in Grade 8, to confabulatin' poems about *crick hockey*?" Uncle Jack protested. "It don't make no sense."

But then, Uncle Jack was not well-informed about feminine Muses, never having been past the Grade 4 curriculum, in his own early school days.

CANADIAN WINTER SONG
By
Leyland Dumfries, aged 12-and-a-half

*

Shinny! Shinny! That's the ticket!
Down on the ice, at Bungman's Crick-et!
So come All Ye Bonny Fair Young Girls and Lissome Maidens and
choose up names!
First Dibs is coming!
And ...
So fare thee quick!
And bring your stick ...
And a puck ....

"*Oi!*" said little Barbara suspiciously. "What's all this '*lissome young maidens*' lurk, then?"

"It's just sort of *nouvelle*," explained Leyland, rather hurt. For it was his first hockey poem, even if a bit unfinished.

"*Puh-lease!*" groaned Leonard Pyle. Then Leonard Pyle showed Leyland his own recent effort:

O, thou Willows-of-Sadness, so drooping, so thick!
Shedding Willow-Leaf Tears, into Bungman's brown crick!

"Read it and weep, Dumfries," said Leonard with satisfaction. "That's the real McCoy. Smarten up."

But, Leyland was determined to persevere. And it was during that next year that Leyland began his one attempt at a more ambitious longer work, his famous heroic hockey epic:

THE SHINNY-AD
A Hockey Epic in eventually24 Books
By Leyland Dumfries, aged 13
INVOCATION
To the Daughters of Memory
Come Muse!
Do not Abuse!
My lonely wits assist!
As I set forth
Here in the North
My epic lines ~~to list to twist to desist~~ *...*
Surrender now Thy Gifts!
(N.*B. work further on this part, tomorrow.*)

Unfortunately, Leyland's great Hockey Epic never got one line further. The bitter fact was that hockey was not Leyland's *forte*. He was really pretty crummy at all sports in general, as Gillian Fenton advised, so he would never have *one hope in heck* of ever getting the *essence* of shinny. Only girls could do that. And even Leyland's attempts at shorter shinny poems lacked the true hockey essence or *being-ness*, Gilly said.

"Your lines. They don't skate right," criticized Gilly. "They just sort of smack and bumble around."

But Barbara always remained Leyland's comforter and encourager. And there was always his genius crick poetry to fall back upon, Barbara reminded Leyland – that bit about the bees had been grand!

So, still encouraged, Leyland soldiered on. And before he was 17, he had filled his old school scribblers with three collections of poetry, celebrating local cricks and a few lovely cow-ponds - his *Legends of Bungman's Crick, Bungman's Crick in Winter,* and his last real effort, *A Crick Remembered.*

Probably Leyland's happiest success, during his locally well-known crick-poetry period, was his short opus, *Late Autumn Along the Crick,* which won the Norm Pocock Memorial Medal for the Junior Arts over at Pocock Collegiate, when Leyland was 15. Leonard Pyle was furious. But it was a proud morning, when Leyland read out his prize-winner before the whole school.

LATE IN AUTUMN ALONG THE CRICK
By
Leyland Dumfries aged 15

Along our brown crick,
Soon snow will fall thick,
And coldly cover the ground.
Hark, Hark! Some squirrels remark,
Winter is coming to town!
No time to bide.
Our nuts we must hide,
Under some leaning, stream-side trees,
Amid the buzzing of some bees!

"They're hiding their nuts, eh?" said a loud voice.

"*Gillian Fenton*! Report to the Principal's Office, right after Assembly!"

But as the end of his school days approached, it became apparent to Leyland, and to Uncle Jack, that probably Crick Poetry, while excellent, would never provide the boy with a secure occupation.

"Sure, it's a noble undertaking," said Uncle Jack, "as no one's ever tackled the subject properly before. But the boy won't be able to raise a family on it."

"Now, don't be too harsh, Jack," said Martha Hodgson, the pretty widow whom Uncle Jack was courting. "He's still trying to find the essence of himself, Mr. Crouch says."

"That boy wouldn't know *an essence* if it smacked him right on the ear," Uncle Jack grumbled. "And he's still goin' on about bloody bumble bees!"

"Now *there's* a possible idea, Jack," mused Martha. "You might get Leyland a few bee hives and …"

"*Whoa*! I ain't having no bees around here! Stingin' the cows and …"

For the truth was, Jack was afraid of bees.

"Well, maybe later he could take over some of your farm."

"Well, I would. But perhaps, some day I might have to provide for some little 'uns of my own… Mrs. Hodgson."

Martha Hodgson blushed bright scarlet. "Oh dear, yes … Oh dear, my goodness, I suppose you *will* have to find poor Leyland something else then…perhaps …"

But what else could Leyland do in life? Although Mr. Crouch had aroused in Leyland a yearning to be a poet, *The Harvest Basket of Golden Verse* was the only meagre resource rural children had to learn or copy from in those early days.

Barbara had been much more richly endowed, being born right in the inner streets of London England, where Queen Victoria lived! The very literary heart of Our Empire! And when still only a teeny-tiny urchin with a dirty face, Barbara had been trotted off to an elite Infant School on the Lancastrian model.

"Blimey!" Barbara said. "It weren't half noisy!"

But that incredibly cultured background explained why Barbara knew not only *The Decline and Whatsit*, but also many other great

English literary masterpieces, such as W. Shakespeare, and Marks and Spencer's *Faerie Queen.*

"You read *that?*"

"Course we did."

"*No!* Teeny-tiny children in England read *that - in nursery school?*"

"Course we did. We 'ad a whackin' great picture-book, wif all that old fairy lark in' it, didn't we? *Muvfer Goose* — Old Cinders and Bob Thumb and all that lot, weren't it?"

But despite his backwoods deprivation, Leyland Dumfries *did* go on at last, to find his own true *essence,* a steady and reliable *centre* for his particular life, even if it was not in Poetry or Shinny-playing, the two main competitors for the Canadian soul and being-ness!

-But *list!* we are getting ahead of ourselves. For our story today is only about the Young Leyland. So we must return to his early days, now to 1892, when Barbara and Leyland attended the new collegiate institute over in neighbouring Mt. Pocock — bicycling over together on their new Whippet safety bicycles every morning in springtime and autumn; or, as snowy winter came, hitching up Barbara's pet goat, Ellis, to an old toboggan. (Ellis knew his own way home.)

And on one particular Saturday morning in the winter of 1892, we might have found Leyland on the dirt main street of Gormley Centre, going into a familiar shop.

ALF BANTRY

HIGH-CLASS SHOE-MAKING - REPAIRS - SKATE-
SHARPENING

"'Allo, young Leyland," said Alf, taking some tacks out of his mouth and setting down his tacking hammer. "The girl's in the back, with her mum."

But just then Flo Bantry and Barbara came out into the shop with a big wicker basket full of speed-skating blades, with leather straps. Alf had sharpened those blades earlier.

"'Allo, Leyland, love," said Flo Bantry. "Come for your hockey skates, is it?"

"Course he *didn't!*" said Barbara sharply, giving her mother a severe look. For everybody knew that Leyland was a rotten skater and absolutely hopeless at hockey – and, sad to tell, not hugely better at poetry, either.

"We're just goin' over to the fairground, an't we, Leyland?" said Barbara. "To see the Ice-Skating Show."

"Is Ellis coming?"

"Can't. - E's in disgrace. 'E ate one of Mrs. Overton's new button-boots, didn't 'e, Dad?"

Barbara quickly undid her pinafore and hurried to get ready, because that very winter afternoon was the annual Gormley Centre All-Girls-Only Figure-Skating and Ice-Racing Festival! Each winter, the Volunteer Fire Department flooded the old harness-racing track down at the fairgrounds, to convert it for winter into a slick ladies' speed-skating oval, with a separate, snow-banked rink for the figure-skating.

In those days, Gormley Centre Fairground was the premier trotting track in the western part of the province, because in 1882 it had been fitted out for night racing - when that circuit was first illuminated by those new electrical lights invented by Mr. Edison – who had personally installed a small steam-generator in the Judging Barn, just in time for the Fall Agricultural Show, as a gift to his cousins and other relatives in the area.

"Well now, Tom, bless me, aren't you staying for the poultry judging? Apple pie and cream up at the house, afterwards. Your favourite."

"Like to, but we're lighting up Manhattan on Monday."

But this day, ten years later, was the Saturday of the annual Girls-Only-Annual-Skating-Festival, which begins with fancy figure-skating displays by the little girls of the village – then climaxes excitingly with a Speed-Skating Relay Race of the township's most daring young ladies! Then the local folks go over to the Anglican Church basement for a Community Supper – and finally all the community returns to the fairgrounds at 10 pm, for a Family and Friends Midnight Skate, with the skaters all bearing lighted lanterns and candles - a marvellously magical scene in the dark winter night, especially when the moon is full.

"Come on, Leyland!!" called Barbara, as they ran to the fairground that winter afternoon.

The skating show is a highly-skilled display. For in Gormley Centre, as in any proper Canadian small town, every teeny-tiny little girl of any moral character is already a wizard figure-skater by the age of seven. And all the bigger, more veteran girls and young ladies would be coming out today, too.

"Do little children skate in England where Queen Victoria lives, Barbara?"

"Silly! – '*Blimey*! Our lot got to try ice-sliding only that once, didn't we? When that big royal park froze up, over west. Kensington Palace. But Princess Louise run us off with a broom, for scarin' the swans and ducks."

Leyland and Barbara soon arrived at the fairground and rushed to see the skate-changing shed, where all the girls were excitedly strapping or screwing on their sharpened blades.

"*Hey! Girls only*!" warned Gilly Fenton, catching Tom Faulds trying to sneak in with his married sister's figure-skating blades.

This year, the Secret Six would not be performing Figures, because they were currently converting themselves into a daring, advanced, modern young ladies' speed-skating team. Next year, they were planning to go on a professional money-racing-circuit in the U.S., Aileen said. After that, the girls were going to build their own air-ship and go to Brazil!

By one p.m., all Gormley Centre had gathered at the fairgrounds, everyone standing around the freshly flooded rink, stamping their feet and blowing on their hands in the frosty air.

"Seems like a bigger show than last," said Jack, to the widow Hodgson – as Uncle Jack had definitely decided to give up his bachelor ways and get himself married.

"It definitely seems bigger this year, Jack" said Mrs. Martha Hodgson, patting Uncle Jack's gloved hand.

"I'd say it *does* seem bigger, in fact," commented Jack, "Mrs. Hodgson."

"It certainly does seem so … Jack."

Jack was on his best behaviour, because he knew that Martha Hodgson, like most fluffy, soft-hearted females, *adored* figure-skating and such. Jack himself couldn't really see the point – but being a gentleman, figured he'd best pretend.

"Keep the peace," said Jack. "That's mostly ninety-nine percent of the trick in marriage, boy."

"Is that true?" asked Leyland.

"So they say," said Jack. "Haven't tried it yet myself – but I'm gonna."

Some truly elegant exhibitions of artistical figure-skating were displayed that afternoon at Gormley Centre, the teeny-tinnies in cute little fairy costumes and thick woollen tights, being especially charming.

"Oh, aren't they *sweet*!" exclaimed Mrs. Martha Hodgson. "Just like little fairies!"

Even Jack had to admit the teeny-tiny part of the business was uncomfortably touching. When one sweet little girl, Becky Forsythe, age 8, casually tossed off a triple Lutz, followed by a neat toe loop and a suicide spin, Jack almost became emotional. (Little Becky was a fourth cousin, on Jack's mother's side.)

"Jack MacFarland!" chided Mrs. Martha Hodgson. "What's *that* in your eye?"

"Snowflake. Got under the lid," growled Jack. "Lend us a lace-embroidered hankie there … Martha."

It was probably that hidden MacFarland tenderness that decided Martha Hodgson to say "Yes", when Jack proposed, later that afternoon. And a few years later, Jack and Martha were blessed with two little fairy skaters of their own, little Maude and little Adelaide; then later, Jackie Jr. - Plug MacFarland's father.

By the end of the show, Jack was converted. "Jeez!" he said. "These girls can skate! Next, they'll all wanta be playin' hockey!"

But finally came the most exciting, thrilling event of the afternoon, the dangerous and reckless Speed-Skating Suicide Challenge Race for Daring, Modern Young Ladies! A competitive six lap relay event!

"Best stand clear, Martha."

"- 'urry up, Leyland!" exclaimed Barbara. "Else we won't get a good place, will we?"

"Coming," said Leyland, leaving Uncle Jack and Mrs. Hodgson, and following Barbara over towards the judges' stand and the starting line, where they could see the race better.

But who should Leyland and Barbara bump right into, in the jostling crowd, but the Secret Six! - Already dangerously kitted out in their new, daring, modern, racing outfits –heading for the starting line- and all wearing knickerbocker *pants!* They looked brilliant. Aileen Baird was particularly glamorous in her racing-breeks, with blue wool stockings, and a new hand-knitted Fair Isle sweater, which had just arrived from her old Grannie, in Scotland. Her brilliant red hair was tied up, for speed, in a streaming, white silk scarf.

Leyland's sensitive heart fluttered.

"*Oh, my goodness gracious, ladies! Just look who's here!*" exclaimed Jeannie Clarke. "It's that little cutie-pie-sweetheart, Leyland Dumfries!"

"*Gosh!* swooned Amy Dutton. "*Be still, my heart.*"

"*Crikes*, hands off, Dutton. He's *mine* today!" claimed Annie McTavish, grabbing Leyland's collar. "First dibs!"

"You didn't call choosing up, McTavish!"

"I did."

"You did not!"

"Get your greedy paws off Mine Intended, Annie McTavish," challenged Aylie Baird, wrapping her arms around Leyland and pulling him tightly to the bosom of her new Fair Isle sweater. Leyland was almost smothered.

"*OI!*" said an indignant little voice.

Aileen Baird turned. Her face went pale, and she put up her mitten hands, defensively.

"Hey, gosh, sorry, Barbara - we were only just fooling," she said, with a worried look.

"Yeah," said the rest of the Secret Six, backing away.

"We're not looking for any trouble."

"Then take a ...*huh* ...*huh* ... *hike*, then!" warned little Barbara, packing a snowball. "*Eh?*"

"Okay, okay, we're going!"

And the Secret Six quickly, anxiously, backed away.

"That should sort '*er*," Barbara said.

Leyland was astonished. "How did you *do* that!" he asked.

But Leyland already knew the answer. Barbara was from the inner streets of London England, where Queen Victoria lived, so knew how to handle her small mitts.

"You *got* to, don't you? Else you get done. - *Cor!*"

"Do you think Queen Victoria can handle her dukes too?"

"Course she can. What you 'fink?"

"I didn't know royal ladies could do that."

"They *'ave* to, don't they? Else they'd get done too."

But suddenly the spectators erupted into surprised cheering as the racers appeared! For the crowd now learned that coming out today to defend Gormley, would be none other than the daring Aileen Baird and the Secret Six! And racing against them would be the Morpeth Corners Bible Club! Last year's county champions!

The Judges of the race scrambled to take up their places on the reviewing stand, and the traditional challenges were given out:

"Who comes forward today," called out Mr. Allen Crouch through his cardboard megaphone, "to defend the honour and ancient privilege of Morpeth Corners?"

"*We do!*" responded the Morpeth Bible Club. "*God and My Right!*"

"And who comes here to uphold … er … Gormley Centre?"

"*Us!*" shouted the Secret Six.

"Right! Good show. Then let the … competition … no, sorry, contest… um … get started!" ordered Mr. Allen Crouch.

Another loud cheer! For the home crowd now saw that Aileen Baird herself would lead off for Gormley - expected to break away fast, and to establish a strong lead for her team-mates! But racing against Aylie today would be that brilliant Morpeth Corners teenager, Ginnie Greenaway, the greatest young athlete in Western Ontario! The crowd could hardly restrain itself, as the two first racers stepped up to the starting line!

"Go it, the Morpeths!"

"*Barbara!*"

"Ladies! Starting pair! - At the … um …Ready!" called out Mr. Allen Crouch, raising his starter's pistol.

Ginnie Greenaway and Aileen Baird took up their classic lateral stances, knees bent and elbows flared, ready for the gun!

"One! ... Two!... *Three*!"

The starting pistol *cracked*! – and the two heroic girls were off! Down the half-stretch they raced! But hardly had they sprinted neck-and-neck into the first turn, when Aylie Baird lost an edge and, shockingly, went sliding headfirst into a snowbank, near the watering cart!

"Oh, *no*!" cried the partisan crowd.

Well ... the match was already lost. Ginnie Greenaway had gained three-quarters of a lap before Aileen could get back onto her skates in pursuit. The Gormley girls could never make up the gap, even when Amy Dutton tried to trip up Tammy Tamworth, at the final exchange.

Never was there such anti-climax in Gormley Centre.

"Oh, nice one, *Baird*!" accused Lorna Thompson.

"It wasn't my fault, Thompson! Something went wrong with my skate, eh?"

"Oh, sure, sure!"

"*It did!*"

"Oh, sure!"

Next morning, Aileen's father, Duff Baird, showed up at Alf Bantry's Shoe Repair, holding the offending speed-skate blade in his hand.

"I thought you *sharpened* this damn thing, Bantry," he said in a temper.

"And so I *did*, sir." said Alf, rather offended. "That there object was true and clean when it left the grinder. -In't that so, Barbara? - Barbs?"

"Well, it ain't sharp now!" complained Duff Baird. "Look at it!"

Alf examined the offending skate.

"Right. Blimey, I see your point. Seems like somebody's dragged a horse file across it, don't it? -But that weren't done 'ere!"

he added quickly. "That there skate blade were perfec' when it left my premises, weren't it, Barb? - Barb?"

"Perfect!"

"Your Aileen must've done that. Careless. Put a right ding in it, didn't she?"

"*My daughter!*"

"Alright, alright. Fair's fair, so just to keep down any bad feelings, there's your ten cents back. But that weren't done 'ere, Mr. Baird. - Were it, Barb? - Barb?"

Well, no one in Gormley Centre ever figured out how the unfortunate damage to Aylie Baird's racing skate could have happened. But luckily the misfortune did not harm Alf Baird's reputation, as he was still top skate-sharpener in the township. Business still flourished.

That was so fortunate for Leyland Dumfries, because when Leyland finished school the next spring, the troubling solution to his future was unexpectedly provided, when Alf Bantry hired Leyland into the trade, as his apprentice.

ALF BANTRY AND APPRENTICE
Shoe-Making - Repairs - Skate Sharpening
Special This Week: Ladies Speed-Skates
Two Skate Blades for the Price of One!
(Note: This Offer Will Not Last)
Also: Re-webbing of Snow-Shoes and Lacrosse Raquettes

Uncle Jack breathed a sigh of relief. Young Leyland was now established in a steady, profitable trade and could plan his future. Because, of course, skate-sharpening is the real money-maker in Canada. And, as Leyland soon learned, there was a lot more money in skate-sharpening, than in crick poetry. Also, to his surprise, handling skates took him to the very *essence* and foundation of our unique Canadian identity. *Just what Mr. Allen Crouch had always challenged the children to do!*

"See," as Plug MacFarland explained a generation later, "there's a lot of people figure ice-hockey is the germ, or true *ur-grund* – like they say in Lambton County - of Canadian identity, eh? But that theory is all horse-feathers, boys."

Because the actual essence and germ of the Canadian identity was never frozen cricks, nor hockey sticks, nor even skates – but *skate-sharpening.*

"*What?* How you figure *that?*"

"Be logical, boys," Plug explains. "How could there even *be* hockey, without somebody *first* inventing a way to sharpen the skates?"

"Hm! Never thought of it that way. That's pretty hard logic to refute."

"Irrefragable," shrugs Plug. "-Whose round?"

Luckily, Leyland never got to hear Plug's bewildering theory, but nonetheless began his apprenticeship in Alf's shop with his mind focussed on the future importance of practising and mastering his new trade.

Barbara had also finished school now and helped in the shop too, wiping and buckling the sharpened skate blades into correct pairs, ready for customer pick-up – or delivering them herself directly to farms and houses, for a small extra fee (one of Leyland's smart new business ideas), with Ellis and a neat little red runner-sled.

But often, Barbara sat watching Leyland, as he was stitching and practicing his awl on an old pair of patched, leather blacksmith's trousers, found in a back cupboard.

"'Ere! You got that one wrong, didn't you?"

"It's hard to learn!"

"Just keep sloggin' away, in't it?" encouraged Barbara, who was always Leyland's most positive supporter. "Like wot old Willard Tennyson said – '*Onward the Five Hundred*', and '*Once More into the Breeches*', weren't it?"

"That's it," said Leyland, so pleased that Barbara and he still shared a love of poetry.

But poetry now had to be secondary for Leyland; for, as a young man making his way in the world, he had to devote most of his time to practical business matters, to secure his future.

Nonetheless, once a week, after the shoe shop had closed at noon on Saturdays, Leyland might still try to scribble off one last hopeful crick poem while there was still daylight – for Leyland had developed a slight myopic squint, as a result of all that close leather stitching.

But every Saturday night, Leyland and Barbara always went to the soda fountain at Albert Fenton's Drugstore on Main Street, for cherry pop.

Flo Bantry was taking notice.

"*Coo*! What you 'fink?" said Flo, jabbing Alf in the ribs.

"Don't go countin' your geese too soon, Flo," said Alf. "They're still young."

After his apprenticeship, Leyland was even made a junior partner in the Bantry Shoe Repair Shop, at the urging of Flo, who had long seen a romantical-type affection between Barbara and Leyland – and was hoping for a happy outcome.

Leyland's natural creativity, of course, greatly promoted the shop's business development and expansion. When Leyland was 20, he and Alf got a loan from the Mt. Pocock Reliable Bank, to start a small shoe-making factory, with a staff of three, over at the vacant new industrial park at Mr. Pocock. And that's also when Leyland created the famous *Bantry and Dumfries* company motto, today known so far and wide:

Shoes Well-Fitted to Wear on Your Own Two Feet

The company was small, but slowly expanded. In 1898, *Bantry and Dumfries* acquired a profitable side-line of fashionable English imports. Mr. Allen Crouch, who had made a romantic visit via Grand Trunk Railway to Montreal during his last summer holiday, came back with the news that top-quality English-made Chelsea boots were the real cat's meow in big-city Canadian fashion. And by 1900, *Bantry and* Dumfries had started producing their very own version in the factory, the elastic-sided, top-grain leather *Prince of Wales Dandy Boot*, with two-inch elevated heels - a line which launched the small firm into even greater profits, for all the young blades in North Dunoon were soon rushing to wear *Dandy Boots*, especially after the 1901 royal tour by young Prince George, later Prince of Wales. (*'Vast excitement and adoring crowds everywhere,'* said the Gormley *Bulletin!.)*

"*Hip, hip!*" Barbara managed to shout, as she and Leyland watched the Royal Train roar through Gormley Centre Junction, while they were standing alongside Mr. Allen Crouch and his new fiancée, Miss Adeline de Montfort from Montreal.

"*Did you see him?*" Leyland asked breathlessly.

"Course I did."

There were some rough patches in business in the early years, of course. One time, during a brief depression in 1901, *Bantry and Dumfries* suffered some temporary setback, and Leyland, for a time very low and depressed, cast about for a new commercial idea.

"I never get it right," Leyland said in dejection.

"Ere!" said Barbara. "Wot you got to do, is use your imagination, and to build on your established foundation of expertise, in't it?" (Leyland stared – but Barbara had heard Mr. Tom Edison say exactly this, last time Tom was in the area and happened to be hanging around Alf's shop, waiting for his boots to be re-soled and re-heeled.)

"Bigger leather straps, you mean?"

Barbara sighed. "*Cor!*" she said to herself.

"No. 'Ere!" she said, holding up a Dandy Boot. Then she held up a skate blade and its frame and leather straps.

Leyland scratched his head, not getting it.

"What if you was to put some'fing *like this,*" she hinted, "bolted right permanent onto the *bottom* of *this boot*? Instead of 'avin' to strap or screw it on each time?" Barbara said, again holding up the Dandy Boot. "So it's more like …" And she then held up the skate blade and jiggled that suggestively a bit.

Barbara did not like to spell out the whole idea, because she always wanted Leyland to think he had come up with things himself. - But actually, it was again Tom Edison, who had idly tossed off this new invention idea, while he was waiting for his work boots to be re-soled. Tom was always poking around the shop and getting in the way, trying to figure out ways to electrify all the shoe-repair tools - because that darned man just could not sit still and read old magazines like other customers, while he was waiting for his boots.

Leyland scratched his head. Then, belatedly, a dim bulb lit up!

"*Of course!*" he exclaimed. "We already make the quality leather boot! All we have to do is bolt on …!"

"That's it," said Barbara. "Permanent fixed, in't it? So you don't 'ave to strap or screw them on to your shoes every time!" (For in those days, skate blades were still separate from the boots -and had to be attached with clumsy leather straps or screws each time for use.)

Two weeks later Leyland rushed in with the new prototype.

"Look!"

"Wot's that 'fing?" Barbara asked.

"Your new idea!" Leyland exclaimed proudly. "Look – a Dandy Boot, but with these things bolted on the bottom!"

"Them's just *wheels,*" Barbara observed.

"Exactly! Cast-iron!"

Well, as Uncle Jack always said, Leyland was a nice lad, but he never, ever, did quite manage to grasp the *essence* of many things. The new BDM patented rolling-skate never sold well, since all roads and streets in North Dunoon were still either gravelled or dirt, usually ankle-deep in mud, so customers were soon returning the product in dozens. And the BDM was, of course, suicidal on ice.

Nonetheless, now that Leyland Dumfries had become an established young merchant, the time had come for him to think of marriage.

"I'd recommend it," said Uncle Jack, "as female companionship and home cooking is what makes a man's life. -That girl we hired, Bridget, does a smash-up meal at supper-time."

"But I don't know if she'd have me," said Leyland with a worried face.

"Who? *Bridget?*"

"No, no – *Barbara!*"

"Not those reckless Baird or Fenton girls again?"

"Course not ... It's always just ...Barbara."

(God almighty, boy, Uncle Jack said to himself, don't tell me you finally *got it.*)

Uncle Jack was relieved, for he was sure that those daring, advanced, reckless girls, the Secret Six, would one day probably end up in the Kingston Penitentiary for Women. Also, nice boy as Leyland was, Uncle Jack could see that his nephew was too soft and moony to handle advanced, daring, direct modern girls of the 1900's. After all, Leyland was still secretly persevering and writing about buzzy-buzzy humble bees and moony cricks.

But in any event, Aileen Baird had now gone away. She and Gilly Fenton had advance-ordered two of those exciting, new, diamond-framed, chain-drive *Indian* motorcycles, 56 mph, from the new Indian Motorcycle Factory in Springfield, Massachusetts, and had gone away to an Advanced Young Ladies' racing circuit in Ohio. Jeannie Clarke was their team manager and mechanic. And the girls were also still working on inventing an Aerial Flying-Machine, so they could help the next generation of daring young modern ladies to go barnstorming after WWI!

"But I don't know if Barbara would have me," Leyland repeated anxiously.

"Well, probably not," agreed Uncle Jack, "as she's a feisty, independent-minded girl, even if she don't play crick hockey. But you can always give her a try."

Actually, Uncle Jack thought Barbara would be perfect for Leyland. That girl was constant, steady, and true. That girl had sense.

And Jack was right. For not only did the coming of Barbara Bantry into western Ontario hugely improve and straighten out Leyland, but her feisty, positive steadiness helped shape the emerging, new character and genetic pool of the province, as her descendants increased. She even affected local speech patterns. That's why, even today, people in Southwestern Ontario still say 'Playin' 'Ockey', just like Barbara and Wayne Gretzky and the rest of us.

Leyland's first real opportunity to pose the big question came the next Saturday in 1903, the afternoon of the newest Ice-Skating Show.

"An't you comin', Leyland?" Barbara asked.

"Course I will. – Ellis?"

"Oh, 'e ain't goin' this year. 'E don't like it now."

That was because Ellis had gotten into the skate-changing shed last year and eaten two leather skate straps and a horsehair cushion, and it had upset his tummy.

Unlike Uncle Jack with pretty Martha Hodgson, Leyland was too nervous to pop his own big question during the skating events; and then he nervously delayed again, until well after the Pot Luck Supper. The Midnight Community Skate was his last chance to get down to the very essence of the matter.

"Barbara …," he timidly ventured, as he and Barbara were holding hands – knitted wool mittens, really – and clumsily skating round the moonlit oval in the winter darkness. They themselves were not carrying lighted candles, because Ellis had also eaten those, earlier – which was good, because Barbara could not see the awkwardness on Leyland's face.

"Barbara …" he ventured again. "Barbara …"

"Course I will," said Barbara.

Barbara and Leyland were married on the 24th of May, the old Queen's Birthday. The happy couple had an open-air, springtime wedding at Jack and Martha's, with picnic supper after, down on the banks of Bungman's Crick. All the little birds and other foresty-type creatures were chirping and singing joyfully in the willow trees. Barbara was a beautiful little bride, wearing her mother's wedding dress, which Flo had brought with them in their steamer trunks and boxes from London England (where Queen Victoria used to live – but she was dead now.) Alf Bantry gave away the Bride – but nearly missed the ceremony, because Ellis had found Alf's best Sunday suit airing on the clothes-line. Fortunately, Alf and Jack were nearly the same size, so Jack's second best was got out of the mothballs just in time. Little Maude and little Adelaide MacFarland were the flower girls, and Jackie Jr., Plug MacFarland's father, the ring bearer. ("Oh, aren't they ever so sweet!" said Martha MacFarland, handing Uncle Jack her lace-embroidered hanky.) Amy Dutton, Lorna Andrews and Annie McTavish were the Bridesmaids – and Gilly Fenton, Jeannie Clarke, and Aileen telegraphed Best Wishes, from Dayton, Ohio, where they were competing in the Dayton Dirt Track Young

Ladies Motorcycle Trials for Daring Modern Girls. Henry Ford sponsored that event. Tom Edison did the electrical lighting.

"And do you, Barbara Gertrude Bantry, take this man to be your ..."

"Course I do," said Barbara.

When tossing her bridal bouquet to the bridesmaids, little Barbara whipped it so hard that it smacked Amy Dutton right on the nose!

"That should sort *'er*, as well," muttered Barbara to herself. Then she added, "*Sor-ry!*", for Barbara was of course inevitably becoming Canadian.

During the wedding supper, everyone gathered around trestle tables, sheltered by the deep shade and trailing curtains of the willow trees. A small neighbourhood gang of local squirrels and wrens were gathered with great interest, overhead. Bridget had baked the wedding cake. Martha MacFarland made the potato salad. Leonard Pyle, as Best Man, was called upon to give the Toast to the Bride and Groom – but he just read out one of his own poems instead. Mr. Allen Crouch and his fiancée, Miss Adeline de Montfort from Montreal, handed out the wedding presents.

Later, very, very late that night, with a pale moon still glimmering on the low western horizon, and after all the guests had gone home, Leyland and Barbara returned through the meadows and sat closely together on a horse blanket on the bankside, holding hands beside slow-flowing, muddy old Bungman's Crick, where Leyland and Barbara's journey had all begun, listening to the night birds and watching the slow clouds drifting across the sky.

But even although he had now finally awakened and discovered his own true essence, his true partner in life, Leyland was still uncertain.

"Barbara ..." asked Leyland, "did you always want to marry me?"

"What you *fffff* ... no, *thhh* ... *thhh* ...*think*?" said Barbara, lovingly, with a small bridal blush. "And wasn't you always my best friend?"

Meanwhile, up at the house, Ellis was eating the remainder of the wedding cake and a pair of Uncle Jack's best suspenders. Someone had forgotten to shut the screen door.

"Barbara ... did you always love me, even when we were little children?"

For a moment, Barbara thought of picking up a stone and winging it right at Leyland's ear.

But instead, she just said:

"Course I did."

*

Leyland and Barbara lived the rest of their happy lives together in Gormley Centre. Leyland still took a long time to finish finding the rest of himself and squaring up and settling down, as is the case with any young Canadian boy who does not play hockey very well. But it was Barbara who truly blossomed.

It was not long before Lorna Andrews, Amy Dutton and Annie McTavish adopted Barbara, and those four girls together first founded the famous Gormley Centre Fastball Team, *The Gormley Rockets,* down at the ball diamond of the old fair grounds. Everyone was stunned at how quickly little Barbara picked up the American game! Soon she was not only batting .350 and leading the township league, but pitching a wicked fastball!

It was apparent that little Barbara was mightily talented!

"Barbara," said Lorna Thompson in some awe, "why didn't you play sport in London England, where Queen Victoria used to live?"

"*Cor!* ... Our lot didn't 'ave the chance, did we? We just played conkers and a few rounders up our alley, didn't we?"

Lorna and Amy were so touched that they soon wanted Barbara, when winter came again, to come down to Bungman's Creek with them, to try crick hockey. But Barbara never was willing to show herself at *that* game, as she never wanted to do anything that might show up Leyland.

But hockey evolution and human progress is not completed in one generation. For it was not Barbara, but little Flora Dumfries, Leyland and Barbara's small flashing daughter, who later burst out as the most brilliant girls' hockey player in Southwestern Ontario in the early twentieth century – and clearly it was Barbara's genes at work there.

Leyland's influence was more at work in their fine, steady son, Willard Tennyson Dumfries, who like his dad never showed more than average ability in hockey, but later did grow up to become Associate Professor of Romantic Literature at the University of Western Ontario. For the country was expanding - and new opportunities were developing, even for young men, besides chopping down trees. Through love of poetry and hard work, Willard and his generation now had advantages which earlier rural and small-town boys could never have aspired to - such as having a warm indoor job during winter.

In 1904, Aileen Baird, Gillian Fenton, and Jeannie Clarke came home from their daring adventures. They never did complete their air-ship or navigate it to Brazil, because they had become far too homesick for winter ice skating and shinny playing. So they came home - and along with Amy Dutton, Lorna Thompson and Annie McTavish, soon formed a proper reckless young married ladies' hockey team – the *Gormley Centre Lightnings* - adding Nancy Faulds, Tom Faulds' sister, as their goal-tender. (Tom Edison thought up their team name.)

Ginnie Greenaway soon countered by organizing the Morpeth Corners Bible Club into a fierce shinny team as well - and for years the local competition between the two teams was ferocious.

"Pure female-war-on-ice!" warned Uncle Jack, wincing. "Keep clear, eh?"

"Jack MacFarland!" chided Martha.

In the next era, of course, the torch of shinny advancement was passed on; and by the 1920's, it was that reckless and daring little Flora Dumfries who was now the most admired and heroic girl in all Gormley Centre, carrying forward her generation.

It was Aileen Baird who taught little Flora her hockey skills, before Aileen had a little girl of her own (little Fiona.)

"*Go it, the Gormley Girls!*" cheered Barbara. Little Flora scored 4 goals in her first game against Morpeth Corners, and 3 against Glumley. Addy and Maudie MacFarland got a pair each. No one was surprised, because as Gilly Fenton had once insightfully said, "Hockey is really a girls' sport."

But Gillian Fenton actually liked boys too – and adored little Jackie MacFarland, who was a tiny member of Gilly's Sunday School Class. She bought little Jackie his first pair of double-bladed Bob Skates and taught him how to zoom up and down the crick, and then how to do slappers and risers and corner-elbows. Uncle Jack encouraged this – as he himself had never learned to play hockey, being too busy from the age of 11 chopping down bloody trees. Besides, Jack was also very soft on Gilly, as she was a niece of Martha - and Jack was always tender on anything to do with Martha.

"We're *married*. What the hell do you expect?"

In 1905, Aileen Baird married Tom Faulds. Tom was also a leader in the advancement of progressive Western Ontario culture. It was Tom Faulds who broke the barrier that prevented boys and young men from being allowed to figure skate. For in those early days, there was a *terrible* discrimination against boys in the figure-skating world. Aileen and Tom Fauld's son, Ronny, in fact, was the first boy ever to compete in the Gormley Centre All-Girls-Only Figure Skating Festival – winning the prize for Top Boy Skater that year, largely because he was the only boy entered.

Time had passed. The country was moving on, finding its true essence.

But some traditions do not change. That is why still today, on a summer's day down by the banks of old, slow-moving Bungman's Creek, the little birds and other foresty-type creatures still chirp and sing joyfully in the willow trees; the little black squirrels still frolic and bash up one another in the upper branches. And when winter comes to Gormley Centre and to Bungman's Crick, that old muddy stream is again magically transformed into a hard-frozen, shining mirror, where daring girls and doughty boys flash down the shining ice on knife-edged skates - and still put out their rubber boots for goal posts for an old-time game of crick shinny. And so, in the small towns and rural townships, you can still hear, ringing through the frosty air, those classic calls to traditional hockey action:

"First dibs!"

"Hey! I called first!"

"No, you didn't, Tiffany Lawson!"

"Yes, I did, Alisha Patel!"

"Girls! Let's just play!"

"You keep out of this, Jennifer Wong!"

"No fair!"

And still today, on one particular late night in wintry February, down at the old Gormley Centre Fairground, shadow figures of families can still be seen, bearing lighted candle-lanterns that glow magically in the darkness, majestically gliding and sweeping the old oval of the trotting track, under the ancient radiance of a full-shining Ontario moon.

"An't you comin'? - Leyland? Flora? Willard?"

"Course we are. - Where's Ellis? Be sure to close his gate."

Winter Community. For over in the small towns in frozen winter, glittering snow and ice skating, and the luminous poetry of hockey are still deep ties that bind.

Crick verse, wonderful as it is, and other traditional, small town Ontario summery essences - like fastball, church picnics, campground cooking over pinewood fires, freshwater motor-boat cruising, pickerel fishing, or bare-foot water-skiing at the cottage – can come only a close second.